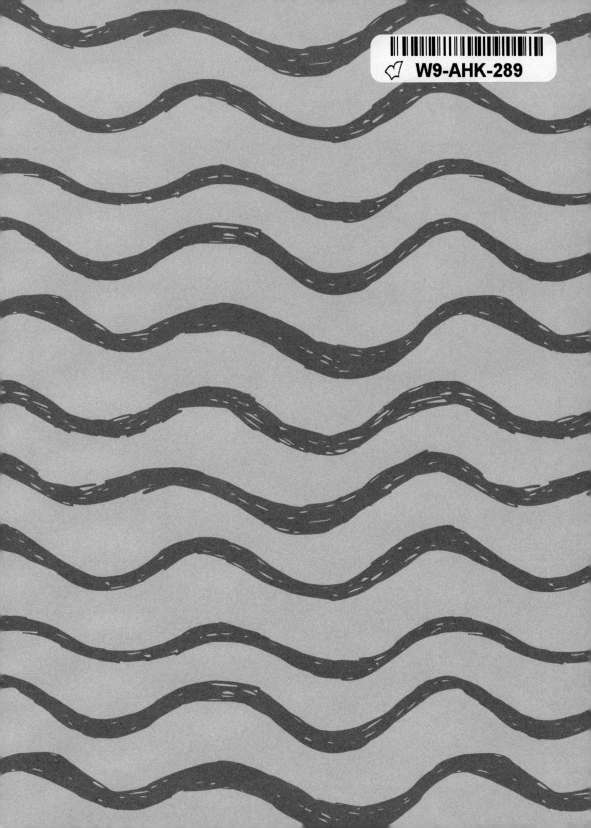

This book
belongs to

....

38 UTTERLY FUNNY STORIES

Compiled by Vic Parker

Miles Kelly

First published in 2017 by Miles Kelly Publishing Ltd
Harding's Barn, Bardfield End Green, Thaxted, Essex, CM6 3PX, UK

2 4 6 8 10 9 7 5 3 1

Publishing Director Belinda Gallagher
Creative Director Jo Cowan
Editorial Director Rosie Neave
Senior Editor Amy Johnson
Senior Designer Rob Hale
Production Elizabeth Collins, Caroline Kelly
Reprographics Stephan Davis, Jennifer Cozens, Thom Allaway

ISBN 978-1-78617-321-8

Printed in China

British Library Cataloguing-in-Publication Data
A catalogue record for this book is available from the British Library

ACKNOWLEDGEMENTS

The publishers would like to thank the following
artists who have contributed to this book:
Advocate Art: Steve Stone (including cover and decorative frames)
Beehive Illustration: Mike Phillips
The Bright Agency: Kathryn Durst, Michael Garton
Milan Illustrations Agency: Tina Perko
Plum Pudding: Mirella Mariani

The publishers would like to thank the following sources
for the use of their photographs:
Shutterstock.com (endpapers) Magnia

Made with paper from a sustainable forest
www.mileskelly.net

CONTENTS

Animal Antics

Fantastic Fools

Trickster Tales

Crazy Capers

Animal Antics

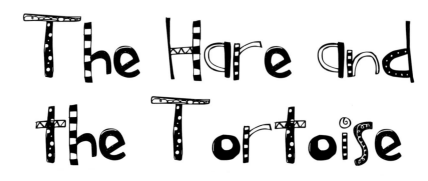

The Hare and the Tortoise

An Aesop's fable

A hare was once boasting to the other animals about how speedy he was.

"No one is faster than me," he said with a smirk. "I challenge anyone to prove me wrong – who is bold enough to race me?"

Of course, no one dared put themselves forward… until a tortoise slowly lifted his head and spoke. "I accept your challenge," the old, wrinkled one announced softly.

The hare burst out laughing. "Oh, that

is funny, please tell me you are joking."

But the tortoise was deadly serious. "Save your boasting until you've beaten me," he replied.

The other animals, astonished, rushed to set a course. It took the tortoise several minutes to amble to the start line. Some of the animals muttered to each other and shook their heads.

"Ready, set, go!" bellowed the ox – and finally the race began.

The hare darted out of sight at once.

As soon as he had rounded the bend, he thought he'd have a laugh at the tortoise's expense. He lay down under a tree and pretended to nap – just to show that he could even stop to sleep and still beat the

tortoise. But in the peaceful shade, the hare really did fall fast asleep!

Slowly, slowly, the tortoise plodded on – past the sleeping hare – until the finish line was in sight. At the sound of the animals' cheers the hare woke with a start, horrified. He bounded on, but the tortoise trudged over the finish line before him.

And the moral of the story is: slow and steady wins the race.

The Elephant's Child

Adapted from the story by Rudyard Kipling

In the High and Far-Off Times, the Elephant, O Best Beloved, had no trunk. He had only a blackish, bulgy nose, as big as a boot, which he could wriggle about from side to side.

There was one Elephant – a new Elephant, an Elephant's Child – who was full of 'satiable curtiosity, and that means he asked ever so many questions.

He filled all Africa with his 'satiable curtiosities. He asked his tall aunt, the Ostrich, why her tail-feathers grew just so, and his tall aunt the Ostrich spanked him with her sharp claws. He asked his tall uncle, the Giraffe, what made his skin spotty, and his tall uncle the Giraffe spanked him with his hard hoof. He asked his broad aunt, the Hippopotamus, why her eyes were red, and his broad aunt the Hippopotamus spanked him with her broad hoof. And he asked his hairy uncle, the Baboon, why melons tasted just so, and his hairy uncle the Baboon spanked him with his hairy paw.

The Elephant's Child

He asked questions about everything that he saw, or heard, or felt, or smelt, or touched, and all his uncles and his aunts spanked him. And still he was full of 'satiable curtiosity!

One fine morning, this 'satiable Elephant's Child asked a fine new question that he had never asked before. He asked, "What does the Crocodile have for dinner?" Then everybody said, "Hush!" and spanked him immediately and directly for a long time.

By and by, when that was finished, he came upon Kolokolo Bird sitting in the middle of a wait-a-bit thornbush, and he said, "My father has spanked me, and my mother has spanked me. All my aunts and uncles have spanked me for my 'satiable curtiosity, and still I want to know what the Crocodile has for dinner!"

Then Kolokolo Bird said, with a mournful cry, "Go to the banks of the great grey-green, greasy Limpopo River, all set about with fever-trees, and find out."

That very next morning, this 'satiable Elephant's Child said to all his dear families, "Goodbye. I am going to the great grey-green, greasy Limpopo River, all set about with fever-trees, to find out what the Crocodile has for dinner." And they all spanked him once more for luck, though he asked them most politely to stop.

Then he went away, a little warm, but not at all astonished, and at last he came to the banks of the great grey-green, greasy Limpopo River, all set about with fever-trees, precisely as Kolokolo Bird had said.

Now you must know and understand, O Best Beloved, that till that very week, and day, and hour, and minute, this 'satiable Elephant's Child had never seen a Crocodile, and did not know what one was like.

He trod on what he thought was a log of wood at the very edge of the great grey-green, greasy Limpopo River, all set about with fever-trees. But it was really the Crocodile, O Best Beloved, and the

Crocodile winked one eye – like this.

"'Scuse me," said the Elephant's Child most politely, "but do you happen to have seen a Crocodile?"

The Crocodile winked the other eye and lifted half his tail out of the mud. The Elephant's Child stepped back most politely as he did not wish to be spanked again.

"Come hither, Little One," said the Crocodile, "for I am the Crocodile." And he wept crocodile-tears to show it was quite true.

Then the Elephant's Child grew all breathless, and panted, and kneeled down on the bank and said, "You are the very person I have been looking for all these long days. Will you please tell me what you have for dinner?"

"Come hither, Little One," said the Crocodile, "and I'll whisper."

So the Elephant's Child put his head down close to the Crocodile's musky, tusky mouth, and the Crocodile caught him by his little nose, which up to that very week, day, hour, and minute, had been no bigger than a boot, though much more useful.

"I think," said the Crocodile – and he said it between his teeth, like this – "I think today I will begin with Elephant's Child!"

At this, O Best Beloved, the Elephant's Child was much annoyed, and he said, speaking through his nose like this, "Led go! You are hurtig be!" Then he sat back on his little haunches, and pulled, and pulled, and pulled, and his nose began to stretch. The Crocodile floundered into the water, making it all creamy with great sweeps of his tail, and he pulled, and pulled, and pulled. And the Elephant's Child spread all his four little legs and pulled, and pulled, and pulled, and his nose kept on stretching – and it hurt him an awful lot!

Suddenly the Elephant's Child felt his legs slipping, and he said through his nose, which was now nearly five feet long, "This is too butch for be!"

Then a Bi-Coloured-Python-Rock-Snake noticed his predicament and knotted himself tight round the hind legs of the scrambling Elephant's Child. He pulled, and the Elephant's Child pulled, and the

Crocodile pulled… but the Elephant's Child and the Bi-Coloured-Python-Rock-Snake pulled hardest. At last the Crocodile let go of the Elephant's Child's nose with a plop that you could hear all up and down the Limpopo River.

The Elephant's Child sat down most hard and sudden. First he said "Thank you" to the Bi-Coloured-Python-Rock-Snake. Next he was kind to his poor stretched nose. He wrapped it all up in cool banana leaves and dangled it in the great grey-green, greasy Limpopo River to cool.

The Elephant's Child sat there for three days waiting for his nose to shrink. But it never grew any shorter, and besides, it made him squint. For, O Best Beloved, you will see and understand that the Crocodile had stretched it out into a really truly trunk same as all Elephants have today. So the Elephant's Child went home across Africa, frisking and whisking his trunk.

One dark evening he arrived back to all his dear families and asked them, "How do you do?"

"Oh bananas!" said they. "What have you done to your nose?"

"I got a new one from the Crocodile on the banks of the great grey-green, greasy Limpopo River," said the Elephant's Child. "I asked him what he had for dinner, and he gave me this to keep."

"It looks very ugly," said his hairy uncle, the Baboon.

"It does," said the Elephant's Child. "But it's very useful." Then that bad Elephant's Child spanked all his dear families for a long time, till they were very warm and greatly astonished.

At last, his dear families went off one by one in a hurry to the banks of the great grey-green, greasy Limpopo River, all set about with fever-trees, to borrow new noses from the Crocodile. When they came back, nobody spanked anybody any more… and ever since that day, O Best Beloved, all Elephants have trunks precisely like the trunk of the 'satiable Elephant's Child.

Brer Bear's House

Adapted from an *Uncle Remus* story
by Joel Chandler Harris

Of all the creatures in the forest, Brer Bear had the biggest and the warmest house. I don't know why or wherefore, but I'm telling you the plain facts, and that's the truth of the matter.

Brer Bear never bragged about it. And even though his house was the biggest, it was still on the small side for his family – who were all rather large! Brer Bear had a

lovely plump wife named Mama Bear and a handsome plump son named Simon and a clever plump daughter named Susanna.

The Bear family always did everything together. They packed into their big dining room to eat together. They jammed into their big bathroom to wash together. They squeezed into their big living room to hang out together. And at nighttime, they squashed into the same big bedroom to sleep together.

Even though they were always treading on each other's toes and jostling each other and stumbling over each other, they loved being a big happy family together in their big warm house.

Now, one day there came a *Bang! Bang! Bang!* at Brer Bear's door. The Bear family looked at each other in surprise. *Bang! Bang! Bang!* The knocking continued – loud and mighty urgent.

Whoever could it be?

"Who's out there?"

growled Brer Bear, just as another *Bang! Bang! Bang!* rattled the door. "Stop bashing at my door, or else!" he roared, his voice like rumbling thunder. "Who are you and what do you want?"

"It's Brer Skunk!" came the answer in a high-pitched squeak. "Please let me in! I was hoping to come and live with you. It's so cold out here! And everyone I meet tells me how warm your big house is. I'll pay my way! I'm a hard worker and you must have lots of jobs that need doing."

Now that, Brer Bear was not expecting. "Hmmm…" he pondered. "It's true that it's mighty cold out there in the forest just now… and it's true that our house is mighty big and mighty warm… but I don't believe you, Brer Skunk. What is it that you're really wanting?"

"Honest, Brer Bear, I'm telling the truth!" came Brer Skunk's voice, his teeth chattering. "I'm such a good housekeeper that lots of forest families have asked me to go and work for them. But you're such a fine gentleman, I'd really most like to work for you."

Brer Skunk's flattery had no effect on sensible Brer Bear. "We don't need a housekeeper," he replied gruffly. "Even if we did, we haven't got room for one. We're short of space as it is. Of course, if you want to keep my house on the outside, you're welcome to do that." He chuckled at his own joke.

But Brer Skunk would not take no for an answer. "Ah," he yelled back straight away, "but I'm so good at clearing up and tidying away that even though you may think you've got no room, I can make you as much space as you want! Just let me in and I'll show you."

Now that got the Bear family thinking. How Mama Bear would love to eat at the dining table without knocking elbows with everyone else. How Susanna Bear dreamed of washing in the bathroom without getting soaked by the others' splashing. How Simon Bear imagined being able to get in and out of bed without bumping into the walls. And how Brer Bear pictured being able to stretch his legs out in the living room instead of sitting cramped in a corner.

"You're hired!" Brer Bear bellowed, and Susanna Bear sprang up to open the door.

Brer Skunk was accompanied in by a bitterly cold wind and swirling leaves. *BAM!* The door slammed shut behind him.

"Now, Brer Bear, let me show you how I can make more space," he said, with a glint in his eye. And he lifted up his bushy tail and squirted his very special scent.

"Bleuuurgh!" the Bear family cried. As the stinking smell filled their noses, everyone began to cough and choke.

Gasping for fresh air, the four bears staggered to the door, threw it open and tumbled outside. They raced off into the forest, trying to get far away from the evil

stench as
quickly as possible.

    Standing in the doorway, Brer Skunk
watched them go with a smirk. Then he
shut the door with a sigh of contentment,
and enjoyed all the space he could have
wished for in the big, warm house.

Taken for a Ride

An extract from *The Talking Horse* by F Anstey

During the Victorian period, some fashionable wealthy people liked to ride horses down Rotten Row, a track in Hyde Park, London. In this story, a young man called Gustavus Pulvertoft wants to join them. He learns to ride, but with unexpected results…

I attended a fashionable riding school near Hyde Park, determined to acquire the art of horsemanship.

To say that I found learning a pleasure would be a lie. I have passed many happier hours than those I spent cantering round four bare whitewashed walls on a snorting horse, with my stirrups crossed upon the saddle. The riding-master informed me from time to time that I was getting on – and I knew instinctively when I was coming off. I must have made some progress however, for as time went on he became more and more encouraging.

I kept on trying and continually asked my riding-master when he thought I should be good enough to go riding in public, down Rotten Row. After a while, he was still not convinced, but didn't actually say no. "It's like this, you see, sir," he explained, "if you get hold of a quiet, steady horse, why, you won't come to no harm, but if you go out on a headstrong animal, Mr Pulvertoft, why, you could get into a spot of trouble, sir."

They would have given me a horse at the school, but I knew most of the animals there, and none of them quite came up to my ideal of a quiet, steady horse. So I went to another stables nearby and asked if they had an animal that might suit me. The stable-master said that he just so happened to have one that would suit me down to the ground.

I thought the horse looked perfect. He was a chestnut of good proportions, with a sleek mane, but what reassured me was the calm look in his eye.

"You won't get a showier park 'orse than what he is, while at the same time

very quiet," said his owner.

I was powerfully drawn towards the horse. He looked very intelligent and he seemed to know that he would have to be on his best behaviour if we rode in front of everyone. With hardly a second thought, I booked him for the following afternoon.

Next day, I mounted at the stables feeling a little nervous. At length, I found myself riding out into the London traffic on the back of the chestnut – whose name, by the way, was Brutus.

I shall never forget the pride and joy of having my steed under perfect control, as we turned into the park. I clucked my tongue and he immediately broke into a canter. I said "Woah" and he stopped.

When I asked him to trot, he trotted. I was so grateful, I could have kissed him!

We had just reached Rotten Row when – and I know you won't believe this – I heard an unfamiliar voice addressing me with, "I say – you there!"

The next moment, I realized it was coming from my horse! I am not ashamed to admit that I nearly fell off. I was too busy trying to get my balance to reply straight away, so the horse spoke again. "I say," he inquired, in a rather cheeky tone, "do you think you can ride?"

39

I looked round in helpless bewilderment. Everything looked normal – and yet, there was I on the back of a horse that had just inquired whether I thought I could ride!

"I have had two dozen lessons at a riding school," I said at last, trying to sound confident.

"I should hardly have suspected it," was his brutal retort. "You are clearly one of the most hopeless cases I've ever met."

I was deeply hurt. "I thought we were getting on so nicely together," I faltered.

All he said in reply was, "Did you?"

"Do you know," I began, trying to be friendly, "I have never ridden a horse that talked before."

"You are enough to make any horse

talk," he answered, "but I suppose I am an exception to the rule."

"I think you must be," I said. "As you are obviously a very special horse, I understand that I made a dreadful mistake in riding you and, if you have the goodness to stand still, I will get off at once."

"Not so fast," he said. "I have long been looking out for an owner who would not overwork me," said the horse. "I want you to buy me."

"No," I gasped in shock. "You must excuse me," I blustered, "I don't want to buy a horse, and with your kind permission, I will spend the rest of the day on foot."

"You will do nothing of the sort," replied the horse.

"If you won't stop and let me get off properly," I said with distinct firmness, "I shall roll off onto the ground."

"I will bolt away with you first," the horse replied. "You must see that you are in my power. Come, now – buy me!"

I had an idea. "If you take me back then, I will arrange it at once," I said.

Needless to say, my plan was to get safely off his back, after which nothing was going to make me buy him.

But, as we were heading back to the stables, the horse said thoughtfully, "I think it will be better if you make your offer to my owner before you dismount."

I was too vexed to speak – this clever animal had outwitted me!

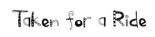

When we clattered into the stable yard I
tried to slip off, but Brutus instantly jogged
my memory and gave a little
buck. Then he quickly backed

into the centre of the yard, stamping
obstinately. "I like this horse so much," I
called out to the stable-master, as I clung to
the reins, "that I want to know if you
would possibly sell him to me."

Here, Brutus became calm and attentive.

"Well, step into my office, sir," said the delighted stable-master, "and we'll talk."

Of course, I would have been only too willing to get off, but the suspicious animal would not hear of it – he immediately began to turn round and round.

"Let us settle it now – here," I said, gripping on anxiously, "I can't wait."

The stable-master grinned at my urgency. "Well, we won't haggle, sir. Why don't we call it an even hundred."

I had no choice – I had to call it a hundred. I took him.

Anansi the Spider Goes in Search of Common Sense

An Afro-Caribbean myth

Anansi the Spider was a trickster, full of mischief. One hot day, he had what he thought was a good idea. No, not a good idea – a great idea. No, not a great idea – a wonderful idea. An idea so incredibly clever and cunning that his eyes sparkled with excitement.

Anansi was going to get some common sense. Not a little bit of common sense, or even a lot of common sense – but all the common sense in the world. After all, if Anansi was the only creature with any common sense, everyone would have to come to him for advice. When they did, of course Anansi would generously share his wisdom – but charge dearly for it. How powerful Anansi would be! And how rich! He chuckled with delight at the thought.

Anansi scrutinized all the gourd trees round about until he found one growing an enormous, firm, hard-skinned fruit called a calabash. He picked the calabash, cut the

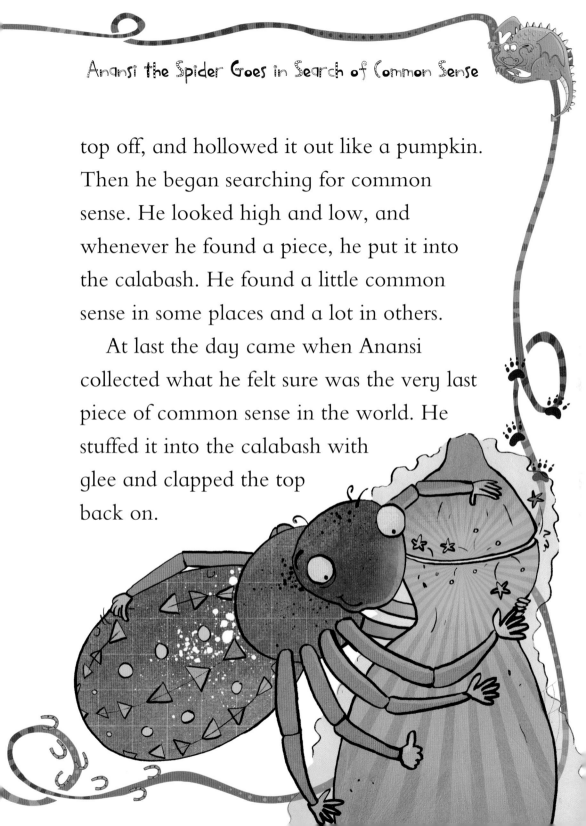

top off, and hollowed it out like a pumpkin. Then he began searching for common sense. He looked high and low, and whenever he found a piece, he put it into the calabash. He found a little common sense in some places and a lot in others.

At last the day came when Anansi collected what he felt sure was the very last piece of common sense in the world. He stuffed it into the calabash with glee and clapped the top back on.

'There! Now all I need to do is find a secret place to keep my precious treasure,' Anansi thought, looking around eagerly. His eyes fell on a very tall, very slender tree. "Perfect," he breathed, squinting up at the very top.

Anansi fetched a length of thick rope and attached both ends of it to the enormous calabash. Then he knotted the rope around his neck so the calabash dangled in front of him like a giant locket on a necklace. How uncomfortable it was! The rope cut into Anansi's neck and the calabash bashed into his stomach at his every move. Nevertheless, Anansi began determinedly to climb the tree.

Oof! It was hard work. Anansi was far

from his usual nimble self, with the big bulky calabash between himself and the tree. His fingers scrabbled to keep hold, his many legs trembled with the strain, his stomach ached with the bruising weight of the calabash pressed against it, and his neck burned from the rope.

Still, Anansi tried to keep his mind on being powerful and rich… and huffing and puffing, slipping and gripping, humping and bumping, up he went, little by little.

Anansi had climbed just over halfway up the tree when he heard someone giggling below him. He looked down and saw a young girl peering up at him.

"Oi! What are you laughing at?" Anansi shouted angrily.

"You!" sniggered the little girl. "Why on earth are you trying to climb with that calabash in front of you? If you had hung it behind you, so it dangled down your back, it would have been so much easier!"

Anansi couldn't believe his ears. How could he have missed that piece of common sense? If he'd missed that piece, how many more pieces had he missed? The thought filled Anansi with fury and frustration, and he lost his temper completely.

"Aaaaiiiiieeeee!" he screeched in a rage. He tore the rope from around his neck, and with all his might, threw the calabash away from him. Down… down… down it fell…

Crash! It hit the ground with an almighty thud and shattered. The pieces of common

sense spilled out, and were caught up by the
wind and blown all over the world. That is
why, today, there is common sense
everywhere, for us all to share.

Mouse Deer and Tiger

A Southeast Asian folk tale

Mouse deer are common in South and Southeast Asian rainforests. A mouse deer is slightly larger than a domestic cat. Its legs and tail are like a deer's, but its face resembles that of a mouse. It features in many folk tales as a very cunning creature.

Once upon a time, there lived a cunning mouse deer in a big rainforest. He was so sharp-witted that all the other animals in the rainforest used to come to him with their problems, asking for his advice. So the mouse deer had many friends. However, he also had some enemies. His worst enemy was the ever-hungry tiger.

One day, the mouse deer was snoozing in the shade under his favourite tree when the tiger came stalking silently by, hunting for food. The tiger had not eaten for many days and his stomach was on fire. His eyes lit up when he saw the sleeping little mouse deer – he could hardly believe his luck. Awake, the mouse deer was very fleet of foot and extremely difficult to catch. He was also silver-tongued and had tricked him more times than the tiger cared to remember. But now, the tiger could almost taste the delicious morsel waiting for him.

He licked his lips – but the very light smack of his tongue against his teeth was

all it took to wake the sharp-eared mouse deer. The little animal sprang up, instantly alert. He started in fright at the sight of the tiger's golden eyes, staring out at him from the undergrowth, and he leapt away at once. With a roar of frustration, the tiger made a mighty pounce and just managed to grab hold of the mouse deer's hoof.

"Aha! Now at last I have you!" the tiger growled delightedly. "And don't even think about trying to talk me out of eating you. You've conned me with your tall tales a million times before and I am not going to fall for your trickery again!"

"Fair enough," said the little mouse deer coolly, although inside he was trembling with fear. "But I'm warning you, once you've eaten me, don't even consider tasting that delicious cake over there." The mouse deer indicated a brown, roughly circular mound nearby, which he well knew was really a pile of monkey poo that had become mixed with some dried leaves. "That is a special cake that belongs to the king himself," the mouse deer continued.

"He ordered me to guard it and not let any animals in the forest taste it."

"But you weren't guarding it, you were sleeping," snarled the tiger gleefully. "I think I might go and tell the king, so he can punish you before I eat you."

"Oh, Mr Tiger, please don't do that," the mouse deer begged. "I'll tell you what, if you don't tell the king that I was sleeping, I will let you try the cake – just a teeny weeny bit. It must really be delicious if the king wants to keep it all to himself."

The tiger's stomach growled and he eyed the special cake greedily.

"Just let me walk a few steps away to the river over there," urged the mouse deer. "Then if the king's guards happen to pass by while you're tasting the cake, I can tell them that I was dying of thirst and really had to go for a drink – and perhaps the king will excuse me."

"Um – alright, I suppose so…" said the tiger, whose brain was befuddled by thoughts of the delicious cake. He released the mouse deer's hoof and the little creature ran away as fast as he could.

Of course, as soon as the tiger bit into the 'cake' he knew at once he had been tricked. "BLEUUURGH!" he yelled, spitting out the mouthful. Howling with rage, he sprang away into the rainforest after the mouse deer.

The tiger screeched to a halt when he found the little creature standing next to a wasps' nest. "Now, don't go telling me that's the king's new hat," snarled the tiger. "That's a wasps' nest, I know it is, so don't bother trying to fool me."

To the tiger's surprise, the mouse deer gave a little giggle. "The king's new hat!" he chuckled. "Anyone can see it's not the king's new hat. But you can't seriously think it's a wasps' nest." The mouse deer lowered his voice and whispered secretively, "Don't go telling anyone now – it's the king's new drum."

"The king's new drum? It doesn't look like one," answered the tiger uncertainly.

"That's because it's a special new kind of drum – the king doesn't want anyone to have one but him," announced the mouse

deer. "The king doesn't even want anyone else to play this one," he continued, "but… I suppose it wouldn't hurt to let you have just one go, Tiger, to prove to you that it really is a drum."

"I agree," said the foolish tiger, "you've tricked me so many times that I refuse to believe this really is the king's new drum until I beat it for myself."

"Very well," replied the little mouse deer, "but I don't like the sound. It's much too loud for my sensitive ears. Let me stand among those trees over there."

"Alright," said the tiger, picking up a nearby stick.

Of course, the moment that the tiger hit the 'drum', wasps came buzzing out in an

angry swarm and began stinging him all over. "OW! OW! OW!" screeched the tiger, running away as fast as he could to escape the furious insects.

In fact, he ran so fast and so far that the cunning little mouse deer never saw him in that part of the rainforest again.

The Reluctant Dragon

Adapted from the story by Kenneth Grahame

One evening long ago, a little shepherd boy was driving his flock home across the wide green ocean of the hills when he came across a dragon, lying half out of a cave. The dragon was as big as four carthorses and covered with shiny blue scales. As he breathed, little flames flickered up over his nostrils. He had his chin on his paws and appeared to be enjoying the cool of the evening. He was even purring!

The boy had read lots of fairy stories and knew all about dragons, so he wasn't afraid. "Hello dragon," he said – quietly, so as not to surprise the monster.

The dragon made to rise politely, but when he saw it was a boy he said severely: "Now don't you start throwing stones at me, or squirting water, or anything. I won't have it!"

"I'm not going to," said the boy, dropping onto the grass beside the beast. "I was just wondering how you were. But if I'm disturbing you, I can easily clear off."

"No, please don't go off in a huff,"

replied the dragon hastily. "I've not been here long – I do like it, but the fact is, it's a trifle dull at times."

The boy chewed on a stalk of grass. "Going to stay?" he inquired.

"I can't say," replied the dragon thoughtfully. "I am confoundedly lazy! The other fellows are always rampaging and skirmishing and chasing knights and devouring damsels. All I want is a meal and a snooze now and then, and plenty of time to think up poetry. On the whole, I feel quite inclined to settle down here…"

"The only problem being," said the boy, "that you're an enemy of the human race."

"I haven't got an enemy in the world," said the dragon. "Too lazy to make them!"

"Oh dear," sighed the boy. "Listen – when other people find out you're here, they'll come after you with spears and swords. According to their thinking, you're a baneful monster!"

"Not a word of truth in it," said the dragon, wagging his head solemnly. "Now, do you want to hear that sonnet I was composing when you arrived?"

"If you won't be sensible," said the boy, getting up, "I'm off home. I'll look you up tomorrow. In the meantime, do try and realize that you're a pestilential scourge and you should leave, or you'll find yourself in a most awful fix. Goodnight!"

After that, the boy spent many a pleasant evening sitting with the dragon,

listening to him recite story-poems of
days gone by, when dragons were quite
plentiful. However, what the boy
had feared soon came
to pass…

A morning came when
the boy walked into the
village to find bunting
and flowers hanging
everywhere. The villagers
were lined up along both
sides of the little high
street, jostling each
other. The boy hailed
a friend. "What's up?"
he cried. "Is it travelling
players, or a circus, or what?"

"Haven't you heard? There's a real live dragon in a cave in the hills!" replied his friend. "St George is coming to slay the deadly beast!"

Just then cheering broke out as a great warhorse pranced down the street, carrying St George in gleaming golden armour. The saint halted his horse in front of the inn, assured the cheering villagers that all would be well, then dismounted and strode confidently inside.

The boy made off up the hill as fast as he could go.

"The game's up, dragon!" he shouted as soon as he was within sight of the beast. "St George is here, and he's got the longest, wickedest-looking spear you ever did see!"

"Oh deary me," moaned the dragon. "You must tell him to go away. He can write if he likes, but I can't give him an interview. No offence to him – I'm not seeing anybody at present."

"Now dragon," implored the boy, "you've got to fight him, 'cos he's St George and you're the dragon. Better get it over with, and then we can go on with the story-poems."

"My dear little man," said the dragon solemnly, "I've never fought in my life and I'm not going to begin now. Just run down and make it alright, there's a dear chap."

So the boy rushed back to the village and burst into the inn, where St George was musing over his chances of winning.

"St George," panted the boy, "there's been a misunderstanding. This dragon is a good dragon. He's a friend of mine and tells the most beautiful story-poems."

"Draw up a chair," said St George. "I like a fellow who sticks up for his friends, and I'm sure the dragon has his good qualities. But are you absolutely certain there isn't some hapless princess tied up within yonder gloomy cavern?"

"I assure you, St George," the boy said earnestly, "there's nothing of the sort. The dragon's a real gentleman."

"Even if you're right," objected St George, "the rules say that the dragon and I have to fight."

"Well, why don't you at least meet the dragon for yourself and talk it over?" suggested the boy.

St George thought for a moment. "Well, it's irregular," he mused, "but it sounds sensible…" And off they strode together.

The dragon woke with a start as the pair approached.

"This is St George," introduced the boy. "St George, meet the dragon."

"So glad to meet you, St George,"

began the dragon, rather nervously, "I've heard a lot about you…"

"Now dragon," said St George pleasantly, "let's come to a business-like arrangement. Why don't we just fight it out and let the best man win?"

71

"But St George," the dragon protested, "the whole thing's nonsense. There's nothing to fight about. I'm simply not going to. If you try to make me, I shall just go into my cave and retire down a deep hole there until you get sick of sitting outside waiting for me."

St George gazed at the landscape around them. "But this would be such a beautiful place for a fight," he implored. "These great rolling hills for the arena, and me in my golden armour against your blue scaly coils! Think what a picture it would make!"

"Well, I suppose it would…" the imaginative dragon agreed, wavering.

"I could spear you somewhere it wouldn't hurt… under these folds of thick skin on your neck, for instance. You'd never even know I'd done it!" declared St George. "Then afterwards I'd lead you to the marketplace. I'd explain that you've seen the error of your ways, and so on. And then there would be the usual banquet."

"Well…" said the dragon, "I suppose I am bored up here, and I would indeed like to go into society. So…"

"Right, that's settled!" said the boy, winking at St George, who took the hint and rose to go.

"I'll even try to breathe fire," the dragon said. "It's surprising how easily one gets out of practice, but I'll do the best I can. Goodnight!"

Early next morning people began

streaming up into the hills in their Sunday clothes, carrying picnic baskets, intent on securing good places for the spectacle. The boy went to sit in the front, well up towards the cave, anxious that the dragon might change his mind and not show up.

Presently, cheering and the waving of handkerchiefs told the boy that St George was coming. Very gallant he looked on his warhorse, his golden armour glinting in the sun, his great spear held tall, its white flag with a red cross fluttering. St George halted his horse and then remained motionless, while the spectators watched in breathless expectation.

"Now then, dragon!" muttered the boy, fidgeting. But he needn't have worried.

The Reluctant Dragon

A low growling, mingled with snorts, rose to a bellowing roar. Then an impressive cloud of smoke obscured the mouth of the cave, and out of it the dragon came splendidly forth. "Ooooh!" everyone gasped. His blue scales glittered, his long spiky tail lashed, his claws tore up the turf, and smoke and fire shot from his nostrils.

"Oh, well done, dragon!" said the boy quietly to himself. "Didn't think he had it in him!"

With both contesters present, the battle began. St George lowered his spear, dug his heels into his horse's sides, and came thundering over the grass as the dragon charged with a roar. There was a moment's entanglement of golden armour with blue coils and spiky tail, and then the great horse, chomping at his bit, carried the saint clear.

"Incredible!" yelled the villagers.

'How well they managed that!' thought the boy.

St George steadied his horse and wiped his brow. Catching sight of the boy, he smiled and nodded. Then he hefted his spear and again galloped towards the dragon, who crouched at his approach, cracking his tail like a whip. The saint wheeled as he neared his opponent and the dragon rose onto his hind legs.

The end was so swift that all the boy saw was a mess of golden armour, spines, claws and flying turf. The dust cleared,

the spectators cheered, and the boy saw that the dragon was pinned to the ground by the spear, St George astride him.

The boy ran towards them breathlessly, hoping the dear old dragon wasn't really hurt. As he approached, the dragon lifted one large eyelid, winked slowly and shut it again.

"Ain't you goin' to cut 'is 'ead off, master?" asked one of the applauding crowd. He had bet on the dragon to win, and naturally felt a trifle annoyed.

"There's no hurry," replied St George pleasantly. "Let's all go down to the village first and have some refreshment!"

He released the dragon, who rose and shook himself and ran his eye over his spikes and scales, to see that they were all in order. Then St George mounted his horse and led him away, in the company of the boy, with the cheering spectators following at a respectful distance behind.

Back in the village, everyone crowded round in front of the inn to hear St George give a speech. He told his audience that he had removed the source of their woe. That the dragon had been thinking things over and didn't want to be their enemy any more, but would like to stay and settle down. He told them that they must all make friends, and the villagers weren't to go thinking they'd got troubles, because they hadn't − besides, next time they'd have to do the fighting themselves.

Then he sat down, amid much cheering. The dragon nudged the boy in the ribs and whispered that he couldn't have said it better himself.

Finally, the banquet was prepared and the feasting began. What fun was had by all! St George was happy because there had been a fight and yet he hadn't had to kill anybody. The dragon proved to be delightful company and was the life and soul of the party. And the boy was happy because his two friends were on the best of terms, and all the villagers were happy too.

As midnight approached, the guests began to drop away with many goodnights and congratulations and invitations, and the dragon wandered out into the street followed by the boy and the saint. The dragon gazed up at the stars. "Jolly night it's been," he murmured.

And they set off up the hill arm-in-arm, the dragon, the boy and the saint.

Henny-penny

Adapted from a traditional tale
told by Joseph Jacobs

One day Henny-penny was pecking at grain in the yard when – *whack!* An acorn fell and hit her upon the head. "Goodness gracious me!" said Henny-penny. "The sky's a-going to fall – I must go and tell the king." Henny-penny was not particularly clever.

So she went along, and she went along, and she went along till she met Cocky-locky. "Where are you going,

Henny-penny?" said Cocky-locky.

"Oh! I'm going to tell the king the sky's a-falling in," said Henny-penny.

"May I come?" said Cocky-locky.

"Certainly," said Henny-penny. So Henny-penny and Cocky-locky went to tell the king the sky was falling in.

They went along, and they went along, and they went along till they met Ducky-daddles. "Where are you going to, Henny-penny and Cocky-locky?" said Ducky-daddles.

"Oh! We're going to tell the king the sky's a-falling in," said Henny-penny and Cocky-locky.

"May I come?" said Ducky-daddles.

"Certainly," said Henny-penny and Cocky-locky. So Henny-penny, Cocky-locky and Ducky-daddles went to tell the king the sky was falling in.

So they went along, and they went along, and they went along till they met Goosey-poosey. "Where are you going to, Henny-penny, Cocky-locky and Ducky-daddles?" said Goosey-poosey.

"Oh! We're going to tell the king the sky's a-falling in," said Henny-penny and Cocky-locky and Ducky-daddles.

"May I come?" said Goosey-poosey.

"Certainly," said Henny-penny, Cocky-locky and Ducky-daddles. So Henny-penny, Cocky-locky, Ducky-daddles and Goosey-poosey went to tell the king the sky was falling in.

So they went along, and they went along, and they went along till they met Turkey-lurkey. "Where are you going, Henny-penny, Cocky-locky, Ducky-daddles and Goosey-poosey?" said Turkey-lurkey.

"Oh! We're going to tell the king the

sky's a-falling in," said Henny-penny, Cocky-locky, Ducky-daddles and Goosey-poosey.

"May I come, Henny-penny, Cocky-locky, Ducky-daddles and Goosey-poosey?" said Turkey-lurkey.

"Why, certainly," said Henny-penny, Cocky-locky, Ducky-daddles and Goosey-poosey. So Henny-penny, Cocky-locky, Ducky-daddles, Goosey-poosey and Turkey-lurkey all went to tell the king the sky was falling in.

So they went along, and they went along, and they went along till they met Foxy-woxy. And Foxy-woxy said to Henny-penny, Cocky-locky, Ducky-daddles, Goosey-poosey and

Turkey-lurkey: "Where are you going, Henny-penny, Cocky-locky, Ducky-daddles, Goosey-poosey and Turkey-lurkey?"

"We're going to tell the king the sky's a-falling in," said Henny-penny, Cocky-locky, Ducky-daddles, Goosey-poosey and Turkey-lurkey.

"Oh! But this is not the way to the king, Henny-penny, Cocky-locky, Ducky-daddles, Goosey-poosey and Turkey-lurkey," said Foxy-woxy. "I know the right way, shall I show you?"

"Why certainly, Foxy-woxy," said Henny-penny, Cocky-locky, Ducky-daddles, Goosey-poosey and Turkey-lurkey. So Henny-penny, Cocky-locky,

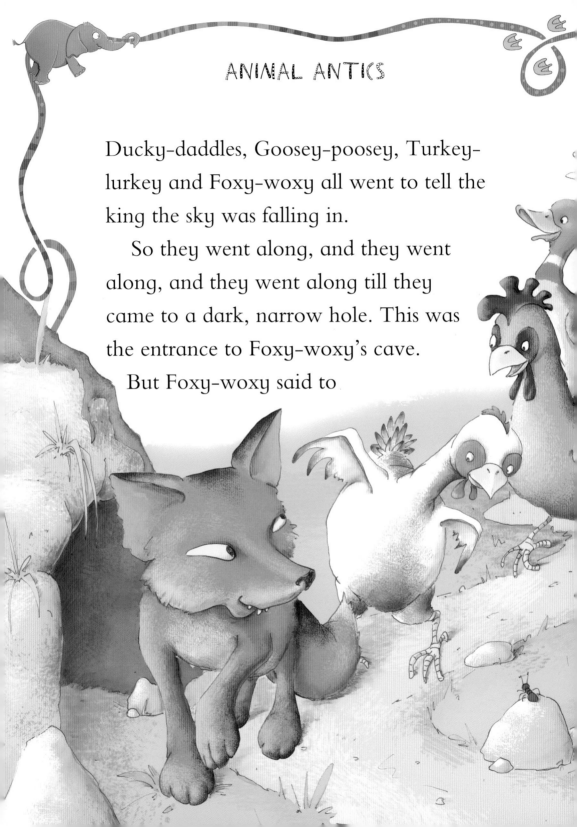

Ducky-daddles, Goosey-poosey, Turkey-lurkey and Foxy-woxy all went to tell the king the sky was falling in.

So they went along, and they went along, and they went along till they came to a dark, narrow hole. This was the entrance to Foxy-woxy's cave.

But Foxy-woxy said to

Henny-penny, Cocky-locky, Ducky-daddles, Goosey-poosey and Turkey-lurkey: "This is the short cut to the king's palace – you'll soon get there if you follow me. I will go first and you come after, Henny-penny, Cocky-locky, Ducky-daddles, Goosey-poosey and Turkey-lurkey."

"Why of course, certainly, why not?" said Henny-Penny, Cocky-locky, Ducky-daddles, Goosey-poosey and Turkey-lurkey.

So Foxy-woxy went into his cave. He didn't go very far, but turned round to wait for Henny-Penny, Cocky-locky, Ducky-daddles, Goosey-poosey and Turkey-lurkey.

First, Turkey-lurkey went through the dark hole into the cave. He hadn't got far when Foxy-woxy grabbed him and gobbled him up! Then Goosey-poosey went in and she was grabbed and gobbled up too. Then Ducky-daddles waddled down, and straight into Foxy-woxy's tummy he went.

Cocky-locky then strutted down into the cave. He hadn't gone far when Foxy-woxy made a grab at him too.

But the cunning Foxy-woxy missed! Seizing his chance, Cocky-locky scuttled back out of the cave as fast as his little legs would carry him, calling out to warn Henny-penny.

So Henny-penny and Cocky-locky

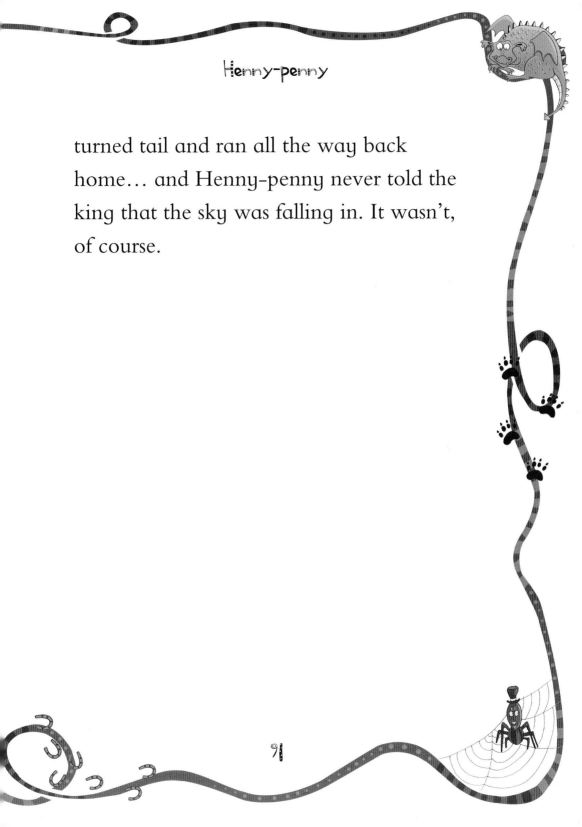

turned tail and ran all the way back home… and Henny-penny never told the king that the sky was falling in. It wasn't, of course.

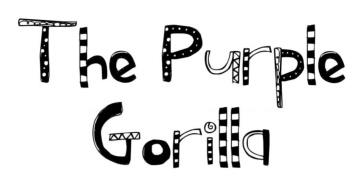

The Purple Gorilla

A North American traditional tale

A boy was cycling down a rough lane through the grassy, treeless prairie where he lived when he saw a turn-off that he hadn't noticed before. Being a curious child with a desire for excitement and adventure, he thought he would take a little detour on his way home and investigate, to see where it led.

No sooner had the boy cycled a little way down the track than the sky began to darken overhead. Heavy black clouds gathered – a storm was coming. As luck would have it, just as the first fat drops of rain began to fall, the boy spotted a house in the distance. He cycled as fast as he could, thinking he would shelter outside on the porch until the storm passed.

As the boy reached the house – *boom!* – the first clap of thunder crashed overhead. He dragged his bike up the steps of the porch and took a moment to catch his breath as the rain came hammering down. When he had recovered himself, he noticed a sign over the front door. In big black letters, it said:

WELCOME — COME ON IN

'That's strange,' thought the boy warily. But his curiosity got the better of him. He tried the door and found it unlocked. So he pushed it open, rather nervously – *creeeeak!* – and stepped inside.

The boy found himself in an ordinary-looking hallway. A coat and umbrella stand stood in the corner, pictures and a mirror hung on the walls, and there were several doors leading off. But it was the door directly ahead, at the far end of the hall, that caught the boy's attention. The door was not wooden like the others but made of heavy steel, and three big metal bolts were keeping it firmly locked. There was another sign on it, which in big black letters read:

The Purple Gorilla

KEEP
OUT

'That looks dangerous,' thought the boy. But his curiosity got the better of him. He crept down the hallway to the steel door, and used both hands to heave back the bolts – *thunk, thunk, thunk* – and push the heavy metal door open – *screeeech!*

KEEP
OUT

Behind the door, a staircase led downwards. 'Now that's just plain creepy,' thought the boy with a shudder. But his curiosity got the better of him. He stepped gingerly onto the first shadowy stair and carefully continued downwards – *squeak, squeak, squeak, squeak!*

At the bottom of the stairs was another sturdy metal door. This one was locked with a bulky chain and enormous padlock – although the key hung on the wall nearby. Another large sign warned:

TURN BACK NOW!
YES, THIS MEANS YOU!

'Me? Really?' thought the boy. But his curiosity got the better of him. He grabbed the key, thrust it into the padlock and turned it hard. It released with a loud and resounding *clunk!*

The boy pulled the door open – *eeeeep* – and stepped into a great big room. In the middle of the great big room there was a great big cage. And in the middle of the great big cage there was a great big purple gorilla. The great big purple gorilla was sitting on a stool with his legs crossed and his arms folded, looking awfully fed up.

DO NOT TOUCH
THE GORILLA!

cautioned an enormous sign hanging over the great big cage.

YOU CAN FEED HIM!
YOU CAN TALK TO HIM!
BUT WHATEVER YOU DO,
DO NOT TOUCH THE GORILLA!
YOU HAVE BEEN WARNED!

'Hmmm…' thought the boy, and his curiosity got the better of him.

A heap of bananas lay in the corner of the room. The boy picked one up and held it out between the bars. To his great surprise, the purple gorilla didn't jump up and snatch it, he reached

out one arm and took it quite lazily. He peeled it precisely and ate it in several dainty mouthfuls, almost as if he was doing it out of politeness. Then, with a heavy sigh, he folded his arms, still and bored once more.

'Well, feeding him wasn't so bad,' thought the boy, letting his curiosity get the better of him. 'Maybe I'll try talking to him.' So the boy said: "Hello, purple gorilla. You do look down. How long have you been here? And why do they keep you behind all these locked doors? What would actually happen if I touched you?"

The boy didn't really expect the purple gorilla to talk back – and of course, he didn't. He just sat there on his stool with his legs crossed and his arms folded, gazing into the distance as if he couldn't hear a word.

Feeling bolder, the boy giggled naughtily and jigged about in front of the cage, pulling a face. But the purple gorilla took no notice at all.

"I wonder…" the boy murmured to himself. He stepped right up close to the bars and thrust his arm through. The purple gorilla didn't even look at him. So the boy raised himself up on tiptoe, pressed himself right up against the bars, reached out at absolute full stretch – and his fingertips just touched the gorilla.

Quick as a flash, the purple gorilla sprang to his feet with a mighty howl and grabbed the bars of his cage. The boy screamed fit to burst. The gorilla began to bend the bars apart with all his might.

The boy didn't wait to see any more. With his heart pounding, he span round and raced for the door.

TOLD YOU SO!

mocked a sign over the door frame as he sped through.

Squeak! Squeak! Squeak! Squeak! The boy took the stairs two at a time as he heard from behind him an almighty *crash!* The purple gorilla had broken the cage apart!

The boy sped back through the steel door, where a sign hanging above it read:

BET YOU WISH NOW YOU HADN'T TOUCHED THE GORILLA!

The boy tore down the hallway, the floor shaking beneath his feet. He glanced over his shoulder to see the purple gorilla striding through the steel door behind him – *thump, thump, thump, thump!*

By the front door, the boy spotted a sign informing him:

THIS IS YOUR OWN FAULT, YOU KNOW!

THIS IS YOUR
OWN FAULT,
YOU KNOW!

With the gorilla hot on his heels, he
sprang through the front door and across
the porch. He grabbed his bicycle and leapt
down the steps, throwing himself astride it
and scrabbling frantically for the pedals.

It was too late. The boy felt the ground
shudder as the purple gorilla charged closer.

Terrified, the boy looked round.

There was the great big purple gorilla standing right behind him. The gorilla reached out his great big hand…

…with his great big fingers…

…and touched the boy lightly on the shoulder. "Tag. You're it," said the gorilla with a grin.

The Man and his Camel

Adapted from a Middle Eastern traditional tale
retold by Horace E Scudder

One cold night, hundreds of years ago, a desert-dweller sat in his tent. He was greatly surprised when a camel thrust the tent flap aside and peered in.

"I beg you, Master," he said, "let me put my head within the tent, for it is so cold here outside under the stars."

"Be my guest," said the desert-dweller. So the camel poked his head into the tent.

The two stayed like that in companionable silence for a while, before the camel politely inquired, "Master, would you be so kind as to allow me to warm my neck also?"

"Of course, do indeed put your neck inside," said the man, so the camel gratefully moved further into the tent.

However, he soon began turning his head from side to side and wriggling uncomfortably. "Master," said the camel, "I don't think it would take up much more room if I put my forelegs inside the tent. It is quite a strain to stretch only my neck inside."

The man nodded graciously. "You may also put your forelegs inside," he said, shifting over a little to make room, for the tent was very small.

But after a while, the camel sighed noisily and said: "Perhaps it would be best

if I stood entirely inside the tent? After all, by standing half-in and half-out like this, I'm keeping the tent flap open and the chill night air is blowing in."

"Yes, yes," said the man. "There's no need for us both to freeze. Why don't you come wholly inside?"

So the camel moved forward until his whole body was inside the tent. His head pushed up against the roof, straining the fabric, and his flanks pressed against the man, so there was not enough space for either of them to even scratch an itch.

"I think," resolved the camel, "that there is not room for both of us in here. It will be best if you stand outside, as you are the smaller of us – there will then be sufficient space for me."

And with that he gave the man a shove, sending him tumbling through the tent flap.

The desert-dweller found himself outside in the freezing desert night, wondering how on earth he had come to end up there…

Fantastic Fools

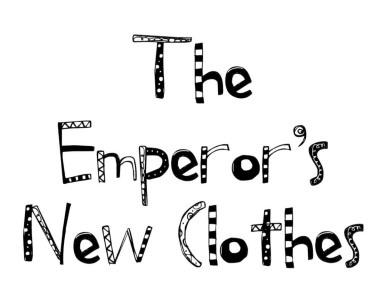

The Emperor's New Clothes

Adapted from the story by Hans Christian Andersen

There was once an emperor who loved new clothes above everything else. Designers, tailors, cloth-makers, dyers, and specialists in all sorts of needlework travelled to his city from all over the world. Anyone who could create flashy, fancy new outfits for the emperor was always very

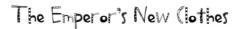

welcome at the palace.

One day, it was the turn of two weavers to be ushered into the emperor's dressing room. The emperor, his butler and all the Officers of the Royal Wardrobe listened in amazement as they described their work.

"We have created a special type of fabric so light and airy the wearer cannot even feel it is there," the first weaver announced proudly.

"Our samples are top secret, which is why we have not brought any to show you," the second weaver explained.

"However, we can assure you that not only are our designs and patterns exquisitely beautiful," continued the first weaver, "but the fabric has a unique

advantage – it is completely invisible to anyone not worthy of his job—"

"—or just plain stupid!" laughed the second weaver, and the emperor and all his courtiers gasped and chuckled along.

"We would be truly honoured if you were to order the very first suit of clothes made out of this extraordinary fabric, Your Imperial Majesty," said the first weaver, bowing low.

The emperor clapped his hands with delight. "I'd like to place an order right away!" he declared, and he gave the two

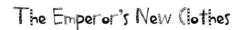

weavers a large sum of money so that they could buy the rare, expensive materials they needed and begin work without delay.

A room in the palace was set aside for the weavers. They set up their looms and got going right away. Meanwhile, news of the strange and incredible cloth spread round the city like wildfire, and soon everyone was talking about it. The weavers worked behind closed doors so no one got even a glimpse of what they were doing. Still, day and night the courtiers and servants in the palace could hear the looms clicking and the shuttles flying – work on the mysterious fabric seemed to be progressing well.

As the days went on, the emperor began

to feel rather uneasy about seeing the cloth for the first time. 'Imagine if I can't see it!' he thought. 'How dreadfully embarrassing that would be!' The worried emperor decided to send his trusted old butler to see how the weavers were getting on. He was sure that his butler was both fit for his job and very wise, and would definitely be able to see the wonderful material.

The weavers bowed low and ushered the butler in. But to the old man's horror, he couldn't see anything at all. 'Heavens above!' the butler thought to himself. 'Those looms look totally bare to me! I must either be a very bad butler, or else I'm an idiot. No one must ever find out…' So he praised the fabric that he could not see,

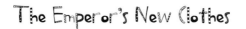

told the emperor that the weavers' work was indeed magnificent, and in due course, everyone in the city heard that the cloth was truly unbelievable.

Soon afterwards, the weavers sent word to the emperor that they needed more money to buy essential items for the work. The emperor had been so delighted with his butler's report that he sent them twice as much money as before.

The emperor was more excited than ever. "I'm going to have the most amazing suit of clothes in the world!" he said to himself ten times a day.

Eventually, just as the impatient emperor thought he was going to explode with anticipation, the weavers announced their

work was finished. They went to the dressing room to present the material to the emperor amid fanfares of trumpets. "Is the cloth not beautiful beyond all imagining?" the weavers sighed.

The emperor smiled a wide smile, trying to hide his horror. The weavers appeared to be holding up nothing but thin air before him. The emperor's worst fear had come true – to him the fabric was invisible!

'I cannot be thought to be a fool or an unworthy ruler,' the despairing emperor thought. So he beamed and leant forwards,

inspecting the air between the weavers'
hands. "Wonderful! Splendid!
Magnificent!" he cried. His butler and all
the Officers of the Royal Wardrobe nodded
and joined him in calling out compliments.
None of them could see anything either,
but they weren't about to risk losing their
jobs by admitting it.

So the weavers got out their tape
measures and their scissors and they set
about cutting the air (so it seemed) into a
pattern. All night long they sewed with
needles that appeared to have no thread,
and in the morning they announced that
the emperor's new clothes were ready.
"Now if Your Imperial Majesty would care
to disrobe, we will dress you in the amazing

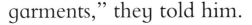

garments," they told him.

The emperor swallowed hard and took off all his clothes. The weavers helped him on with the underpants and trousers and shirt and jacket, all invisible to him. "How do they feel?" they asked him. "Lighter than air?" The emperor spluttered his agreement. He couldn't feel that he had any clothes on at all.

The emperor turned to the mirror. According to what he saw, he didn't have a stitch on! But he turned this way and that, pretending to admire himself. And the butler and all the Officers of the Royal Wardrobe keenly cried out, "How wonderfully the new clothes fit you, Your Majesty!" and "Such amazing colours!"

and "The design is a work of genius!" –
even though it looked to all of them that
the emperor was as naked as the day he
was born.

'Everyone else can see my new suit
except me,' the emperor thought, horrified.
But, summoning his courage, he walked
out of the palace to parade before the
people in his marvellous new clothes.

The streets were lined with hundreds of
people who *ooohed* and *aaahed* and
applauded at the sight of the emperor's new
clothes – for no one wanted to admit that
they couldn't see them.

Suddenly, a shrill little voice rose above
the noise of the crowd. "But the emperor
has nothing on!" a young boy shouted.

"Nothing on at all!"

A stunned silence followed and the boy found hundreds of pairs of eyes staring at him. Then someone sniggered… someone else tried to stifle a giggle… another person let out a snort… and the whole crowd burst into uncontrollable laughter.

The emperor's face turned as red as a ripe tomato. "I am indeed a fool!" he cried. "I have been swindled by two tricksters!" He ran back to the palace as fast as his short, naked legs could carry him – but the clever (and now very rich) weavers were long gone!

The Thunder God Gets Married

A Norse myth

Up in heaven, Thor the thunder god was furious. Someone had stolen his magic hammer, Mijolnir. The hammer was the terror of the gods. Whenever Thor threw it, it killed anything that it touched and then always returned to his hand. Mijolnir was perhaps the most deadly weapon that the gods possessed to protect them against their enemies, the giants.

Now Thor's roars of rage sounded like the clouds were crashing together. His face was so dark with anger that it sent a shadow across the sky. As Thor grabbed blazing lightning bolts and hurled them through the clouds, the mischief-maker god, Loki, came nervously to see him.

"I have good news, my angry friend," Loki explained. "I have used my cunning to find out that it was the giant Thrym who stole your hammer. He has agreed to give it back on one condition – that he has the most beautiful of all the goddesses, Freya, as his bride."

The thunder god's sulky face brightened

a little. He charged off to find Freya straight away. "Put on your best dress, Freya!" Thor boomed, throwing open her wardrobe doors. "You have to marry the giant Thrym so I can get back Mijolnir."

Freya's eyes flickered with cold fire. "Excuse me," she said calmly. "Would you care to repeat that?"

"You-have-to-marry-the-giant-Thrym-so-I-can-get-back-Mijolnir!" the impatient thunder god cried, the words flying from his mouth at top speed.

Freya stood glaring, her hands on her hips. "Firstly, Thor, I don't *have* to do anything."

Thor's face reddened.

"Secondly," Freya continued, "I wouldn't marry that ugly giant if he were the only creature left in the world."

The thunder god hung his head.

"Thirdly," Freya declared, "it's your problem, so you sort it out."

"Sorry, Freya," Thor mumbled, shuffling about a bit. Then he turned and stormed back to Loki. The two gods sat down glumly and wracked their brains to come

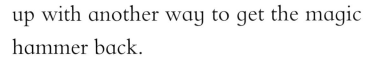

up with another way to get the magic
hammer back.

"How about…" Thor started to suggest.
Then he shook his head. "No, no good."

"What if…" Loki began. Then his face
fell. "No, it would never work."

It looked as if Mijolnir would have to
stay in the land of the giants forever – until
the god Heimdall had an idea.

"That's absolutely out of the question!"
Thor thundered on hearing it.

"Outrageous!" Loki squealed. "I'll never
do it!"

"Well, you come up with another plan
then," Heimdall laughed, knowing that
there wasn't one.

That afternoon, there was great

merriment among the gods and goddesses as they dressed Thor up like a beautiful maiden. How they laughed as they brushed and curled the thunder god's fair hair, and set a coronet of silver and pearls upon his head. They taunted and teased Thor as they adjusted a shimmering gown of Freya's for him to wear, letting out seams and lowering hems, lengthening sleeves and setting in extra panels to make it larger – much larger, for Thor insisted on keeping his chain mail shirt and belt of power on underneath it.

Then finally they draped over the coronet a veil that covered Thor's face. And there the thunder god stood, as beautiful a bride as a giant might wish for.

"I don't know why you're laughing," the furious Thor said to a giggling Loki. "It's your turn next."

And the horrified Loki was given similar treatment by the gods and goddesses until he looked like the perfect bridesmaid for the perfect bride.

As dusk fell that evening, the giant Thrym was delighted to see a chariot with a bride and bridesmaid in it arriving at the castle steps.

"It's Freya!" the gormless giant gasped with delight, as the two figures clambered out. "I shall gladly give back Thor's precious Mijolnir in return for the most beautiful wife in the world!" The overjoyed giant ordered a magnificent wedding

banquet to be prepared and his guests to be sent for at once.

But Thrym wouldn't have been so happy if he could have seen beneath the veils of the bride and bridesmaid, and the angry, highly embarrassed faces of Thor and Loki. As it was, the giant was far too excited – and stupid – to notice how big and clumsy the bride and bridesmaid looked in their delicate dresses. Thrym didn't take in that the women had low, gruff voices and huge hands. And he hardly thought twice about the way that Freya swigged down two whole barrels of beer and devoured an entire roast ox.

When all the guests had eaten and drunk their fill, the beaming Thrym got to his feet to make a speech. "My wife and I," he began, "would like to thank you all for coming here today to celebrate this happy occasion with us. Freya has made me the luckiest being in heaven and Earth. And now, I will keep my word and give back the magic hammer I stole from that ugly thug of a thunder god."

There was a drum roll as one of Thrym's servants brought in Mijolnir on a velvet cushion. Thrym held it high in the air for his marvelling guests to admire, then with a grand flourish, he presented it to his bride.

"The ugly thug of a thunder god thanks you!" roared Thor, ripping off his veil and springing to his feet. He seized the hammer, and before the dismayed Thrym and his guests could really take in the trick, Thor and Loki had disappeared, and the wedding feast was unexpectedly over.

All the gods were truly relieved to have the magic hammer back in Thor's hands in heaven, where it belonged. But it was a

long time before Thor and Loki could laugh with the other gods about how charming they both looked in a dress!

Hans in Luck

Adapted from a traditional tale
by the Brothers Grimm

Once upon a time, there was a young man named Hans who always considered himself to be lucky. He was hard-working too. He laboured for a wealthy man for seven long years, at the end of which the man said, "You have been a faithful and good servant, Hans." And he gave Hans a big lump of silver.

Hans wrapped the piece of silver in his handkerchief, threw it over his shoulder and

set off on the road home. He couldn't wait to see his mother again and show her.

As Hans trudged on, he passed a man trotting along on a fine horse. "Ah," said Hans to himself, "how splendid to ride on horseback like that! If only I didn't have to carry this great lump of silver! It's so heavy I can hardly hold my head up."

The horseman heard it all and his eyes lit up. "My friend, what do you say to an exchange?" he called to Hans. "I will save you the trouble of carrying such a heavy load, and give you my horse for the silver."

"Really? I'll trade most gladly," said

Hans, unable to believe his luck.

So the horseman got off and took the silver, then helped Hans onto the horse and handed him the reins. Hans was extremely pleased and rode off whistling cheerily.

After a time Hans thought he should like to go a little faster, so he cried "Jip!" Away went the horse at full gallop and Hans found himself thrown off. He landed heavily by the roadside. His horse would have run off, if a drover who was coming by with a cow had not stopped it.

Hans picked himself up, most dismayed, and said to the drover, "This riding business is no joke – I could have broken my neck! Your cow is much better than this horse. After all, one can stroll along behind a cow – and she'd give you milk, butter and cheese every day, into the bargain."

"Well," said the drover, "just to help you out I will exchange my cow for your horse, if you like."

"Done!" said Hans merrily. So the drover climbed up onto the horse and away he rode.

Hans continued on, walking his cow towards his mother's village. As noon approached and the heat grew greater, he decided to milk the cow and quench his

thirst. So he tied her to a tree trunk and placed a discarded pail underneath her – but not a drop was to be had! Hans hadn't considered that this cow might be old and past milking.

Just then the uneasy beast grew tired of being bothered and pushed Hans over into a puddle. As luck would have it, a butcher was passing by pushing a pig in a wheelbarrow, and helped Hans up.

"If only my old cow were a pig like yours," sighed Hans. "I may not have milk, but at least I would have sausages."

"Well," said the butcher, "to do a neighbourly thing, I will give you my fine fat pig for your cow."

"May heaven reward you for your

kindness!" said Hans, as he gave the butcher the cow and took the pig.

And on Hans went – until he met a farmer carrying a fine white goose. Hans told the farmer all about his luck and how he had made so many good bargains.

The farmer looked at the pig and sucked in his breath. "I hate to say this, my friend," he said, "but in the village I just came from, the squire has had a pig stolen from his sty. I can't help thinking that's the squire's pig. If it is, and they catch you, the least they will do is throw you into the river. Can you swim?"

"No," cried Hans, very frightened.

"I'll tell you what," said the farmer, "I'll do you a huge favour and take that pig off

your hands, in exchange
for my goose. Not
everyone would do a
good deed like that!"

Hans most willingly
handed the farmer the pig
and took the goose instead.
Then he continued
homewards, free from care,
dreaming of eating roast
goose and sleeping on goose-
feather pillows.

As Hans arrived at the next
village, he saw a scissor-
grinder singing as he worked
at his wheel. Hans looked
on for a while and at last

said, "You seem very happy, sir!"

"Yes," said the scissor-grinder, "I am very well paid for my work. A good grinder never puts his hand into his pocket without finding money in it… but where did you get that beautiful goose?"

"I did not buy it," explained Hans, "I exchanged a pig for it."

"And where did you get the pig?" asked the grinder.

"I gave a cow for it," Hans told him.

"And the cow?" inquired the grinder.

"I gave a horse for it."

"And the horse?"

"I gave a lump of silver as big as my head for it."

"And the silver?"

"Oh! I worked hard for that for seven long years."

"Well, you have had good luck, haven't you?" said the grinder with a wry smile. "Now, if only you could find money in your pocket whenever you put your hand in it, your fortune would be made."

"Very true," agreed Hans, "but how do I manage that?"

"Why, you become a scissor-grinder like myself," replied the grinder. "In fact, I'll give you my grindstone. It's a little bit worse for wear, so I'll let you have it in exchange for your goose."

"I shall be the happiest man in the world to have money in my pocket whenever I put my hand in it," sighed Hans.

So the grinder gave him the rough, worn grindstone that lay by his side, took the plump goose and hurried away.

Hans continued on his way with a light heart. But after a little while he began to grow thirsty – and exhausted from carrying the stone. He dragged himself to the side of the river, to take

a drink of water and rest. He laid the stone carefully on the bank, but as he knelt to drink, he nudged it just a little and down it rolled, *plop* into the stream.

Hans watched it sink. Then suddenly he sprang up and danced for joy. "Thank you heaven," he cried, "for taking away my burden, that heavy stone!"

Then on he walked with a

light heart, free from all his troubles, till he reached his mother's house and told her what a very lucky fellow he was.

The Dragon-tamers

Adapted from the story by E Nesbit

There was once an old, old castle, most of which had crumbled to ruins. Of all its past splendour there were only two little rooms left – and it was here that John the blacksmith had set up his forge. No one asked any rent for the rooms, because all the lords of the castle were dead and gone. So there John blew his bellows and hammered his iron and did all the work that came his way.

John kept his tools and coal in the great dungeon underneath the castle. It was a fine dungeon indeed, with a handsome vaulted roof and iron rings for tying prisoners to. At one end was a broken flight of steps leading down to no one knew where. John himself had never dared to go beyond the seventh step…

One evening, John was busy at his forge while his wife sat and nursed their baby. Presently, over the noise of the bellows and the clank of the iron, there came another sound – like the noise of some great creature purring, purring, purring down below. John took his shovel in one hand and his hammer in the other, hung the old stable lantern on his little finger, and went

down the winding stairs to the dungeon.

Half of the dungeon was empty as usual,
except for his tools and the coal. But the
other side was not empty. It was quite full,
and what it was full of was a dragon.

'It must have come up those broken steps
from goodness knows where,' thought John,
trembling all over, as he tried to creep back
up the winding stairs.

But the dragon shot out a great claw
and caught him by the leg. "No you
don't," the beast said in a deep voice.
"You're the very man I need. Some rivets
have fallen out of one of my wings. Could
you put that to rights?"

John timidly looked the dragon over. He
seemed to be made almost entirely of iron

armour – a sort of tawny, rusty colour it was – and under it he seemed to be covered in fur. Sure enough, his wing was loose.

"You could certainly do with a rivet or two, sir," said John politely. "In fact, you want a good many."

"Well, get to work, then," said the dragon. "You mend my wing, then I'll go and eat up all the town – and if you make a really smart job of it I'll eat you last!"

"Great," said John despairingly. "Would you just let me fasten you up, like I do with horses?"

"Fasten me up?" said the dragon. "How do I know you'd untie me again? Give me something in pledge. What do you value most?"

The Dragon-tamers

At this moment the baby began to cry in the room above. "Bring me your baby," ordered the dragon. "I'll take care of it till you've finished riveting me, and you shall tie me up."

So John ran back up the steps. His wife was asleep, in spite of the baby's cries. John picked up the baby and took him down and put him between the dragon's paws. "Just purr to him," he said, "and he'll be as good as gold." The dragon eyed the baby uncertainly. He began to purr, and his purring pleased the baby so much that he stopped crying.

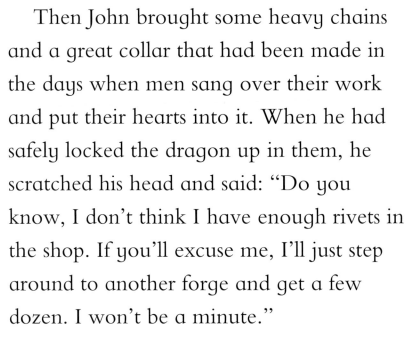

Then John brought some heavy chains and a great collar that had been made in the days when men sang over their work and put their hearts into it. When he had safely locked the dragon up in them, he scratched his head and said: "Do you know, I don't think I have enough rivets in the shop. If you'll excuse me, I'll just step around to another forge and get a few dozen. I won't be a minute."

And off he went, leaving the baby between the dragon's forepaws, laughing and gurgling with pleasure at his purring.

John immediately ran upstairs, shook his wife awake and told her the tale.

"You've given the baby to the dragon!" she cried. "Oh, how could you!"

"Hush," he said, "I'm going back down. After I've been you can go, and if you keep your head the boy will be alright."

So back down the stairs went the blacksmith, and there was the dragon purring away to keep the baby quiet.

"Hurry up, can't you?" he said. "I can't keep up this noise all night."

"I'm very sorry, sir," replied John, "but all the shops are shut. The job must wait till the morning. And don't forget you've promised to take care of the baby. Goodnight, sir." And off he went up the stairs before the dragon could respond.

The dragon had purred till he was quite out of breath – so he stopped. As soon as he did so, the baby started to scream again.

"Oh, dear," said the dragon mournfully, "this is awful." He patted the baby with his claw, but the boy screamed more than ever. Looking around in panic, he noticed a woman sitting on the steps. "I say," he said, "do you know anything about babies?"

"I do, a little," said the woman.

"Then I beg you to take this one and let me get some sleep," implored the dragon, yawning and exposing his sharp teeth.

So John's wife picked up her baby and took him upstairs. She told John what had happened and they went to bed happy, for they had tricked the dragon.

After this, things went a little better for John. To begin with, the baby did not cry quite so much. On top of that, word of the

dragon spread and tourists came from a
long way off, paying twopence each to go
down the steps and have a look at the rusty
dragon in the dungeon.

The baby – named John, after his father
– began presently to grow up. He was great
friends with Tina, the daughter of the
family who lived down the hill. Together,
the children would go and peep into the
dungeon at the dragon, and sometimes they
would hear him mew piteously.

Then one day, people came running into
town screaming that a giant was lumbering
over the marshes towards them.

Johnnie and Tina looked at each other
and then sped off as fast as their boots
would carry them, up to the castle and

down the dungeon steps. They went in and
began to talk casually to the dragon, telling
him what the weather was like outside, and
what there was in the papers. At last,
Johnnie said: "By the way, there's a giant
in the town. He wants you."

"Does he really?" said the dragon,
baring his teeth. "If only I were free, I'd
show him!"

So the children unlocked the dragon
from the chains and collar, and he broke
down one end of the dungeon and went
out – pausing only at the forge door to get
John the blacksmith to fix his wing.

He met the giant at the town gate. The
giant hit the dragon with his club, and the
dragon replied with smoke and fire. It

was a truly fearful sight, but at last the
dragon won and the dejected giant trudged
away again across the marshes. The
dragon, who was now very tired,
went back to his dungeon to sleep
– but not before announcing his
intention of eating the whole
town in the morning.

So Johnnie and Tina
called on all their friends to
help them save the town.

"You must all bring your breakfasts of bread and milk to the forge tomorrow morning," Johnnie and Tina said, and all the children promised.

Next morning, when all the children brought their bread and milk, Tina and Johnnie emptied it into a huge washtub. When the tub was full, with the help of nine other children they carried it down the dungeon steps and called out: "May we come in?"

"Oh, yes," said the dragon, "it's very dull here."

So they went in and set down the washtub next to the dragon. Then the other children went away, and Tina and Johnnie sat on the floor and pretended to cry,

letting out big exaggerated sobs.

"What's this?" asked the dragon. "And what's the matter?"

"There's another giant!" wailed Johnnie. "He's so big he makes the first giant look like a dwarf."

"But he doesn't want to eat us," Tina went on. "He says he'll spare us if he can eat you – with bread sauce."

"That's unfortunate," said the dragon. "And I suppose this sloppy stuff in the tub is the bread sauce?"

The children said it was. "Of course," Johnnie added, "bread sauce is always served with wild dragons. You have to have apple sauce with tame ones, and this giant hates apple sauce. What a pity you're

not a tame one – he'd never want to eat you then."

"Goodbye, poor dragon," said Tina, "this is the last time we will ever see you." And both children began to cry noisily once more.

"Well, look here," said the dragon, "couldn't you tell the giant I am actually a tame dragon you keep for a pet?"

"He'd never believe it," said Johnnie. "If you were a tame dragon you'd be kept tied up, you know."

Then the dragon begged them to fasten him up, and they did so at once and hurried off.

When the captive dragon realized that he'd been tricked, he began to weep. Then

the poor creature dried his eyes and looked about him, and there he saw the tub of bread and milk. 'If giants like this damp, white stuff, perhaps I would like it too,' he thought, and he tasted a little, and liked it so much that he ate it all up.

And the next time tourists came, the dragon asked shyly: "Excuse my troubling you, but could you bring me a little more bread and milk?"

After that, people took the dragon bread and milk every day.

And so ten years passed. Johnnie became mayor, and he and Tina fell in love. On the morning of their wedding they went to see the dragon. He had grown quite tame. His rusty plates had fallen off in places, and

underneath he was soft and furry to stroke. So they stroked him gently.

"I don't know how I could ever have liked eating anything but bread and milk," the dragon said wonderingly. "I am a tame dragon now, aren't I? Won't you undo me at last?"

And Johnnie and Tina were so happy on their wedding day that they unlocked the chains and collar.

As the dragon followed Johnnie and Tina out of the castle into sunshine, he blinked and shook himself. The last of his rusty plates dropped off, his wings with them, and all of a sudden he was just like a very, very oversized cat.

From that day he grew furrier and furrier, and he was the beginning of all cats. Nothing dragon-like remained except the claws, which all cats have still, as you can easily ascertain for

yourself. I hope you see now how important it is to feed your cat with bread and milk. If you were to let it eat nothing but mice and birds it might grow larger and fiercer, and scalier and tailier, and get wings and become the beginning of dragons. Then of course there would be all this bother all over again.

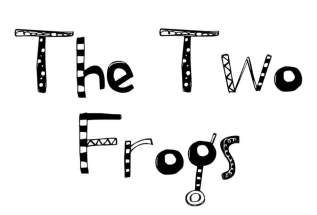

The Two Frogs

A Japanese folk tale retold by Andrew Lang

Once upon a time in the country of Japan there lived two frogs, one of whom made his home in a ditch near the town of Osaka, on the coast, while the other dwelt in a clear little stream that ran through the city of Kioto. At such a great distance apart, they had never heard of each other. But, funnily enough, the idea came into both their heads at once that they should like to see a little of the world.

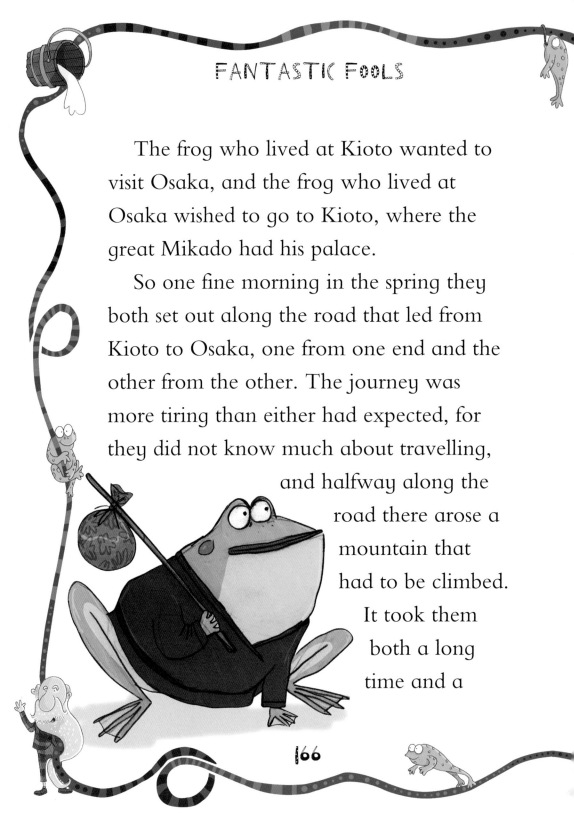

The frog who lived at Kioto wanted to visit Osaka, and the frog who lived at Osaka wished to go to Kioto, where the great Mikado had his palace.

So one fine morning in the spring they both set out along the road that led from Kioto to Osaka, one from one end and the other from the other. The journey was more tiring than either had expected, for they did not know much about travelling, and halfway along the road there arose a mountain that had to be climbed. It took them both a long time and a

166

great many hops to reach the top, but there
they were at last.

Imagine how surprised each frog was to
see another frog before him! They looked
at each other for a moment without
speaking, and then fell into conversation,
discussing the cause of their meeting so far
from their homes. They talked for a long
time, and were delighted to find that they
both had the same wish – to learn a
little more of their native country.
As there was no sort of
hurry, the two frogs
stretched themselves out
in a cool, damp
place and
agreed that

they would have a good rest before they parted to go their separate ways.

"What a pity we are not bigger," said the Osaka frog, "for then we could see both towns from here, and tell if it is worth our while going on."

"Oh, that is easily managed," returned the Kioto frog. "We have only got to stand up on our hind legs, and hold on to each other, and then we can each look at the town we are travelling to."

This idea pleased the Osaka frog so much that he at once jumped up and put his front feet on the shoulders of his friend, who had risen onto his hind legs also. There they both stood, stretching themselves as high as they could and

The Two Frogs

holding each other tightly, so that they
would not fall down.

The Kioto frog turned his nose towards
Osaka, and the Osaka frog turned his nose
towards Kioto. But the foolish creatures
forgot that when they stood up their eyes
lay in the backs of their great heads. So
although their noses were pointing to the

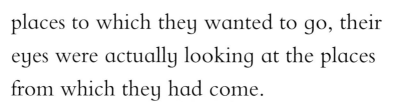

places to which they wanted to go, their eyes were actually looking at the places from which they had come.

"Dear me!" cried the Osaka frog. "Kioto is exactly like Osaka. It is certainly not worth such a long journey. I shall go back home instead!"

"If I had had any idea that Osaka was only a copy of Kioto I should never have travelled all this way," exclaimed the frog from Kioto, and as he spoke he took his feet from his friend's shoulders, and they both fell down on the grass.

Both frogs were disappointed at their discoveries. They took a polite farewell of each other, and set off for home again. And to the end of their lives they believed that Osaka and Kioto – which are as different to look at as two towns can be – were as alike as two peas.

The Milkmaid and her Pail

An Aesop's fable

A farmer's daughter had just completed her morning milking and was carrying a pail of milk from the field to the farmhouse, when it set her thinking. 'When this milk is sold,' she mused, 'the money it fetches will buy at least three hundred eggs. Even allowing for some of the eggs not to hatch, we should end up with at least two hundred and fifty chickens. If we feed and look after the chickens well, they will grow up to achieve the highest price at market.

'So, when they are all sold and Father gives me my share of the proceeds, I shall have enough money to buy a beautiful new gown – maybe even that pink one with rosebuds all over it in the seamstress's window in the village.

'How fabulous I will look in it! I will wear it to every party this Christmas. None of the lads from any of the villages round about will be able to keep their eyes off me. They will all want to talk to me, and dance with me, and even propose to me – but I will toss my head and refuse them, every one of them.'

And with that, she tossed her head vainly and turned on her heel, pretending

to scorn a suitor's hand in marriage. But at the sudden movement, the heavy milk pail slipped from her hand. *Crash!* It fell to the ground and the milk spilled everywhere and ran away – along with all her foolish imaginings…

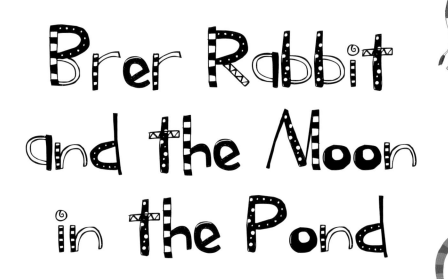

Brer Rabbit and the Moon in the Pond

Adapted from an *Uncle Remus* story
by Joel Chandler Harris

Every now and again Brer Fox and Brer Rabbit would shake hands and make peace for a while and, following their example, all the critters would forget their arguments and get along together just fine and dandy. It had been like this for some weeks when Brer Rabbit ran into Brer

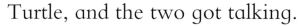

Turtle, and the two got talking.

"It sure is peaceful around here now," sighed Brer Rabbit.

"Yep," nodded Brer Turtle, who was a critter of few words.

"It sure is quiet," sighed Brer Rabbit.

"Yep," nodded Brer Turtle.

"Peaceful and quiet is good, but it ain't fun like in the old days, is it, Brer Turtle?" asked Brer Rabbit.

"Nope," agreed Brer Turtle.

"I think that the folks round here could do with a good dose of fun again," sighed Brer Rabbit.

"Yep," nodded Brer Turtle.

Brer Rabbit bounced to his feet with a chuckle. "Then I'm going to invite

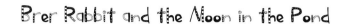

everyone to a little fishing frolic at the pond tomorrow night," he said. "I'll do all the talking as long as you back me up with your 'yep's and 'nope's now and then."

Brer Rabbit and Brer Turtle shook hands in agreement. Brer Rabbit bounded off to do the inviting and Brer Turtle set out for the pond, so he'd be sure to get there on time…

Sure enough, the following night everyone was there at the pond, ready to fish. Brer Bear and Brer Turtle had brought their hooks and lines. Brer Wolf carried a pot of wriggling bait. Brer Fox brought his fishing net. Miss Meadows and Miss Motts brought themselves, dressed up to the nines.

While Brer Wolf shook his pot at

Miss Meadows and Miss Motts and made them squeal with delight, Brer Bear announced he was going to fish for mud-cats. Brer Turtle said he was going to fish for horneyheads. Brer Fox declared he was going to fish for perch for the ladies. And Brer Rabbit winked at Brer Turtle and said he was going to fish for suckers.

So everyone got busy readying their hooks and their lines and their bait, and Brer Rabbit went to the edge of the pond to cast his line first. "I don't believe it!" he gasped, peering into the water and scratching his head. "The moon has gone and fell in the water!"

Everyone looked serious and gathered round and tut-tutted and well-welled and

my-myed as they looked into the pond and saw the moon floating there like a big pale coin. "There ain't no fish gonna come swimmin' through this water unless we get the moon out of the way," said Brer Rabbit. "Isn't that so, Brer Turtle?"

"Yep," nodded Brer Turtle, with a twinkle in his eye.

"So how we gonna get the moon out, Brer Rabbit?" worried Miss Meadows.

"Hmm," pondered Brer Rabbit. "I've got it! We borrow Brer Turtle's drag net, and we drag it across the pond, and we drag the moon right out!"

"That's it!" agreed everyone excitedly. "That's surely it!"

"It don't bother you none if we borrow your drag net, does it, Brer Turtle?" asked Brer Rabbit.

"Nope," replied Brer Turtle, trying hard not to collapse into laughter.

Then Brer Rabbit leapt off to fetch Brer
Turtle's drag net and was back again
before anyone could say 'lickety-spit'. "I
think I'd better be the one to do the
dragging," Brer Rabbit declared. "It needs
someone mighty clever and muscley."

At that, Brer Fox and Brer Bear and
Brer Wolf sprang forward and insisted on
taking the drag net from Brer Rabbit. After
all, they didn't want to look foolish in front
of the ladies, now did they?

Brer Fox and Brer Bear and Brer Wolf
walked gingerly to the edge of the pond
with the net. They cast it into the water,
dragged it along, and heaved it out,
dripping. When the ripples had settled on
the pond, there was the moon, shining just

as bright in the water as before.

"Nope!" cried Brer Rabbit. "You need to go into the pond."

Brer Fox and Brer Bear and Brer Wolf waded knee-deep into the cold pond. Once again they cast out the big drag net, and once again they pulled it in empty.

"Try again, a little deeper," yelled Brer Rabbit from the nice, dry bank. "You'll surely get it next time." Miss Meadows and Miss Motts eagerly waved them further out.

Brer Fox and Brer Bear and Brer Wolf took one more step… and suddenly the bottom of the pond fell away steeply and there was no more mud under their feet and they were ducked right under the water! Up they popped, choking and

splashing and spluttering.

Miss Meadows and Miss Motts and Brer Turtle and Brer Rabbit laughed and laughed, and then laughed some more as Brer Fox and Brer Bear and Brer Wolf hauled themselves out of the pond. They were a sight for sore eyes, dripping water from every bit of fur and covered all over in waterweed.

"I've heard that the moon will always bite if you use fools for bait," Brer Rabbit giggled, looking them up and down with satisfied glee. "Now if you're asking me, you gentlemen ought to hurry yourselves home and get into some dry clothes."

Brer Fox and Brer Bear and Brer Wolf had to grudgingly admit that Brer Rabbit had got the better of them. They slopped and slapped and squelched away into the moonlight.

The Bearded Fool

An Indian fable

Once upon a time there lived a man with a very long beard that reached down past his waist. He was very proud of his beard and washed and combed it every day. 'My long beard makes me look so intelligent, like a professor,' he would think, admiring himself in the mirror.

One evening, the man sat up late, reading by candlelight. He was really enjoying his book – a popular tome of

proverbs and wise sayings – until he came to a sentence that read: "Any man with a long beard is a fool."

'What?' he thought. 'That can't be right – I can't have read that correctly!' And he read the sentence again, very carefully: "Any man with a long beard is a fool."

The man was most dismayed. "But I always thought my long beard made me look so scholarly!" he cried. "I have been wrong all along. And all this time, everyone has been thinking I am a fool!"

The man felt so disappointed and embarrassed that he decided to get rid of his long beard at once. He hunted high and low for a pair of scissors. He knew he had some somewhere, but could he find them –

no. And of course, he hadn't had a razor in the house for a very long time.

Immensely frustrated, the man grabbed the offending hair in his hands and without thinking, thrust the tip over the flame of a candle. It caught fire at once – but the flames licked up the length of his beard much faster than he had expected. In just a moment, the hair was all gone and the fire was singeing his chin. Next, his moustache caught fire. Then a spark leapt up into the hair on his head and that started burning too. "Aaaaiiiiieeeee!" the man screeched. How it hurt! Within moments, the hair on his head was all burnt to ash.

The man's screams of panic brought his neighbours running at once. How shocked

they were to see his scorched face and head, surrounded by little wisps of smoke.

"What on earth happened to you?" they cried, splashing him with water.

"It was destiny," said the man, sadly. "I read that men with long beards were fools, and indeed, I have proved it!"

The Husband Who Was to Mind the House

Adapted from a Norse folk tale told
by Sir George Webbe Dasent

Once upon a time there was a man who
was always surly and cross. He never
thought his wife did anything right in the
house. So one evening, his wife said: "Dear

love, don't be so angry – there's a good
man. Tomorrow let's swap our work. I'll
go out with the harvesters, and you stay
here and mind the house."

The husband thought that would do
very well.

So, early next morning, his wife took a
scythe and went out into the hayfield,
leaving the man to do the housework.

First, the man set to churning the butter.
It was thirsty work, and after a while he
went down to the cellar to tap a barrel of
ale. But, just when he had knocked in the
bung and was putting the tap into the cask,
he heard the pig come into the kitchen
overhead. Off he ran up the cellar steps
with the tap in his hand, as fast as he could.

But by the time he got there, the pig had already knocked over the churn. It stood there, grunting, among the cream – which was running all over the floor.

The man was wild with rage. Then all

at once he remembered he still had the tap in his hand! By the time he got back down to the cellar, every drop of ale had run out of the cask. Furious, he began to churn what cream was left, for they needed butter for dinner. However, when he had churned a bit, he remembered that their milking cow was still shut up in the barn, and hadn't had a bite to eat or a drop to drink all the morning.

'It's too far to take her down to the meadow,' he thought. 'I'll just take her up to the roof to graze,' – for the house was roofed with turf and a fine crop of grass was growing there.

Now their house stood close against a steep hill, and he thought if he laid a plank

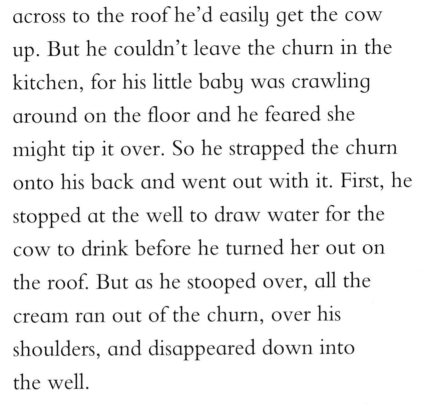

across to the roof he'd easily get the cow up. But he couldn't leave the churn in the kitchen, for his little baby was crawling around on the floor and he feared she might tip it over. So he strapped the churn onto his back and went out with it. First, he stopped at the well to draw water for the cow to drink before he turned her out on the roof. But as he stooped over, all the cream ran out of the churn, over his shoulders, and disappeared down into the well.

It was now nearing dinner-time, so he thought he'd best hurry up and boil the porridge. Once he'd turned out the cow, he filled the pot with water and set it over the fire. When he had done that, he began to

worry that the cow might perhaps fall off the roof. So he got up there to tie her up. He fastened one end of the rope to the cow's collar, and the other he threw down the chimney. Then he went back inside and fastened the loose end around his own leg.

Hurriedly, he began to grind the oatmeal… but while he was at it, down fell the cow off the roof after all! As she fell, she dragged the man up the chimney by the rope, feet first. There he remained, stuck fast. As for the cow, she hung halfway down the wall, swinging between heaven and earth, for she could get neither down nor up.

Now when the wife got home and saw the cow hanging in such a manner, she ran

straight up to the roof and cut the rope in two with her scythe.

Of course, as she did this, down came her husband out of the chimney… so when the wife entered the kitchen, she found him standing on his head in the porridge-pot.

The Celebrated Jumping Frog of Calaveras County

Adapted from the story by Mark Twain

An old friend wrote to me and told me to be sure I made the acquaintance of a neighbour, Simon Wheeler, to ask after my friend's childhood companion, Leonidas W Smiley. So I did – and here's what

happened. I have to say that I now suspect there is no such person as Leonidas W Smiley, that my friend made him up to get old Simon Wheeler to tell me his long, exasperating story about another man called Smiley. If my friend's aim was to fool me into sitting with a man who talks your ears off, then I fell right for it.

I found Simon Wheeler in the tavern, dozing by the fire. He roused at my approach and said good-day. I told him a friend had asked me to inquire about a Leonidas W Smiley.

Immediately, old Simon Wheeler backed me into a corner and trapped me there with his chair. "Well, I can't say I know any Leonidas W Smiley," he began, "but there

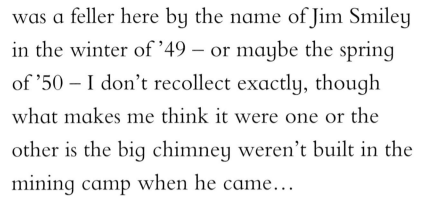

was a feller here by the name of Jim Smiley in the winter of '49 – or maybe the spring of '50 – I don't recollect exactly, though what makes me think it were one or the other is the big chimney weren't built in the mining camp when he came…

"Anyways, he was a gambler through and through – the sorta man who'd bet on anythin', long as he could find someone to bet against him, and if he couldn't, he'd change sides and bet the other way himself. If there was two birds on a fence, he'd bet you which would fly first. If he saw a long-legged straddle-bug beetle start to go somewhere, he'd bet you how long it would take him to get wherever he was going. And if you took him up on the

bet, he would follow that straddle-bug anywheres till he found out where he was going and how long it took – all the way to Mexico, if he had to.

"Lots of the boys here knew Smiley and can tell you 'bout him. He'd bet on anythin'. And Smiley was lucky with it – uncommonly lucky – he always came out on top…

"Well, 'cept for the time Smiley caught a frog. He said he calculated to educate him. He did nothing for three months 'cept sit in his backyard and teach that frog to jump. And you bet he did teach him, too. He'd give him a little nudge behind and next minute you'd see that frog whirling through the air like a doughnut. You'd see him turn

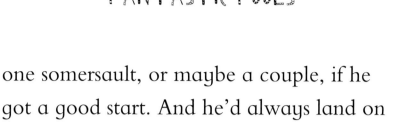

one somersault, or maybe a couple, if he got a good start. And he'd always land on his feet, like a cat. Smiley got him practising catching flies too, until that frog only needed to look at a fly and it was his.

"Smiley said all a frog needed was education and he could do almost anythin' – and I believe him. Why, I've seen him set Dan'l Webster down here on this floor – Dan'l Webster was the frog's name – and sing out, 'Flies, Dan'l, flies!' and quicker than you could wink he'd spring straight up and snake a fly off the counter there. Then he'd flop down again, solid as a gob of mud, and scratch the side of his head with his hind foot as if he'd done no more than any other frog might do.

"You never saw a frog so modest and straightforward as him, for all he was so gifted. And when it came to fair and square jumping on level ground, he could jump further than any other frog in God's creation. Long-jumping on level ground was that frog's speciality, you understand. Smiley was monstrous proud of his frog, and well he might be, for fellers that had travelled and been everywheres all said he was the most amazin' frog they ever saw.

"Now Smiley kept Dan'l Webster in a little box and every now and again he'd bring him out for a bet. One day a feller – a stranger in town – comes across him and says: 'What might it be that you've got in that box?'

"And Smiley says, sorta indifferent-like, 'It's just a frog.'

"And the feller took it, and turned it this way and that, and said, 'Hmm, so 'tis. What's he good for?'

"'Well,' Smiley says, 'he can outjump any frog in Calaveras County.'

"The feller took the box again, took a long look, and then gave it back. 'Well,' he says, 'I don't see nothin' about that frog that's any better than any other frog.'

"'Maybe you don't,' Smiley says. 'Anyways, I'll risk forty dollars that he can outjump any frog in Calaveras County.'

"And the feller thought a minute, and then said, 'Well, I ain't got no frog, but if I had a frog, I'd bet you.'

"Then Smiley says, 'That's alright. If you'll hold my box, I'll go and get you a frog.' And so Smiley went off and the feller waited. He sat there a good while, thinking to himself. Then suddenly he got out a little bag from his pocket – filled with lead shot it was, the smallest kind, the sort you use for hunting quails. He got the frog out of the box, opened his mouth and took a teaspoon and filled him full of lead shot – filled, I tell you! Then he put him down on the ground.

"Meanwhile, Smiley came back with a frog he caught in the swamp. He gives the new frog to this feller and says: 'Now if you're ready, set him right alongside Dan'l, with his forepaws even with Dan'l's, and I'll give the word.' Then he calls out,

'One… two… three… get!' And him and the feller touched the frogs from behind.

"The new frog hopped off lively. But though Dan'l give a heave, he couldn't budge – he was planted as solid as a church! Smiley was a good deal surprised, and he was disgusted too, but he didn't have no idea what the matter was, of course, not a clue. So the feller took Smiley's money, and as he was leaving, he commented casually, 'I still don't see nothin' about that frog that's any better than any other frog.'"

Here Simon Wheeler heard his name called from the tavern's front yard and stood up to see what was wanted. It was nothing important, and so he sat straight back down and began again. "Where was I?" he continued with a grin. "Oh yes, well, this here Smiley also had a yellow, one-eyed cow that didn't have no tail, only just a short stump like a little banana you see, and so Smiley—"

At that, I stood and bid the old
gentleman good-day, and politely took
my leave.

Trickster Tales

Brer Rabbit and the Tar Baby

Retold from an *Uncle Remus* story
by Joel Chandler Harris

Brer Fox was doing what he usually did
– trying to catch Brer Rabbit. But
he'd be danged if this time he didn't catch
that pesky vermint once and for all! Brer
Fox mixed up a big pot of sticky tar and
pulled and patted it into the shape of a
baby. Then he lolloped up the road, set the

tar baby sitting in the dust, and went to lay low in the ditch.

Brer Fox waited… and waited… and waited… and by and by, Brer Rabbit came bouncing down the road. "Good morning," Brer Rabbit greeted the tar baby, "nice day, ain't it?"

The tar baby didn't utter a word.

"I SAID," shouted Brer Rabbit, just in case the tar baby hadn't cleaned his ears recently, "GOOD MORNING! NICE DAY, AIN'T IT?"

The tar baby just stared straight ahead.

"Ain't you got no manners?" Brer Rabbit asked crossly.

Still the tar baby stayed silent.

By this time, Brer Rabbit was hopping

from foot to foot, madder than a snake in a wasps' nest. "You'd better speak to me civil-like or else!" he hollered.

The tar baby ignored Brer Rabbit.

"Well, I guess you've gone and asked for this!" Brer Rabbit shrieked. He drew back his fist and thumped the silent figure straight in the mouth. But Brer Rabbit didn't realize that his enemy was made of sticky tar. His fist sunk deep into it and stuck fast in the tar baby's face. Brer Rabbit pulled and pulled and pulled – but he couldn't free his fist even an inch.

"You let me go!" Brer Rabbit yelled. "Let me go – or I'll let you have another!"

But the tar baby did not let go.

"Don't say I didn't warn you!" yelled

Brer Rabbit and the Tar Baby

Brer Rabbit and – *BAM!* – he socked the
tar baby again. His other fist sank into its
head and also stuck fast.

"Right, you've asked for this!" bellowed
Brer Rabbit. *SMACK!* He kicked the tar
baby, saw his foot disappear into the
soft black gloop, and was left
hopping around on one leg.

"Don't push me!" Brer
Rabbit shouted. *WALLOP!*
Another kick and his
other foot sank into
the gooey tar.
Now the tar baby
was holding him
off the ground.

"I'll give you one

last chance to let me go!" Brer Rabbit hollered. "I mean it! If you don't release me, I'll make you pay, good and proper."

But the tar baby didn't utter a sound and didn't move a muscle.

"No? Really! Right, you've had it now!" Brer Rabbit screamed. *THUNK!* He head-butted the tar baby and found himself stuck eye-to-eye with the cheeky critter.

All this time, Brer Fox had been holding in so much laughter he thought he was going to burst. Now he leapt out of his hiding place and cried, "My oh my, Brer Rabbit! What kind of mess have you got yourself into this time?"

"I suppose you're gonna have yourself a tasty barbecued bunny for supper this

evening," Brer Rabbit admitted.

"Yep! You said it," grinned Brer Fox, licking his lips.

"Well, I'm glad you're going to dress me up with some sauce and warm me over your fire," Brer Rabbit smiled. "I'd much rather you did that than throw me in that briar patch over there."

'Hang on a minute,' thought Brer Fox, his face falling, 'that no-good rabbit seems quite pleased about being roasted!'

"I've changed my mind," Brer Fox said out loud. "I'm gonna hang you instead."

"Ain't I glad it's a good old hangin' and not being thrown in the briar patch!" sighed Brer Rabbit.

Brer Fox frowned. "I mean, I'm gonna

drown you!" he declared.

"Fine, fine…" replied Brer Rabbit lightly. "Dip me in the water and at least I'll die clean. Just don't throw me in that there briar patch, that's all!"

Brer Fox was then sure that the very worst thing he could do to Brer Rabbit was to hurl him into the prickly briar patch. He grabbed him round the waist and pulled him hard, and – *shlup!* – Brer Rabbit came unstuck from the tar baby. Holding him tightly, Brer Fox spun round and round and round and – *wheeeee!* – Brer Rabbit went sailing high into the air and came down – *thump!* – in the briar patch.

Brer Fox's face broke into a

broad grin. "I've bested that bunny once and for all!" he chuckled, wiping his hands.

But a high-pitched giggle came from the far side of the briar patch. When Brer Fox squinted into the sunshine, he could just see Brer Rabbit hopping away into the distance. "I was born and bred in a briar

patch, Brer Fox!" he was singing gleefully. "Hee hee! Born and bred in a briar patch!"

Filled with rage, Brer Fox thumped the very first thing that came to hand. And you know what that was, don't you?

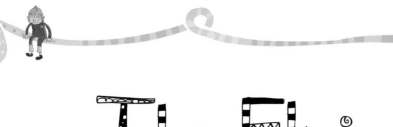

The Flying Trunk

Adapted from the story
by Hans Christian Andersen

There was once a clever merchant who made so much money that he could have paved a street with gold. When he died, his son inherited his wealth – but unfortunately not the merchant's good sense. The young man lived a merry life, squandering all his riches until at last he had nothing left but the clothes he stood in and four shillings.

Of course, all his so-called friends deserted him. One of them even mocked him by sending him an old trunk with the message: "Pack up and get lost!"

"I would," the young man sighed, "if I had anything left to pack up. Maybe I should just pack myself up…" He climbed into the trunk and sat there, fiddling with the lock.

To his great amazement, as he pressed on it he felt a sudden jolt upwards. For the trunk was magic and flew away when anyone pressed the lock. Now it rocketed up the chimney and into the sky. It soared through the clouds, all the way to Turkey, where it gently came to rest in the middle of a wood.

When the trunk was no longer moving, the young man clambered out. Tingling with excitement, he hid the trunk under some dry leaves and made his way to a nearby city. The streets were bustling with people. The young man spotted a mighty palace rising above the other buildings. He introduced himself to a passer-by and asked who lived there.

"Why, the sultan's daughter lives there," the woman replied. "It has been foretold that she will fall in love with a trickster, and therefore no one is allowed to visit her unless the king and queen are present."

"Thank you," said the merchant's son. He thought for a while, then hurried back to the wood, seated himself in the trunk

and flew up to the roof of the palace. He crept through a window into the princess's room, where she lay sleeping.

As he stood watching her, she woke up and was very frightened. The young man told a fib – he said he was an angel who had come down from heaven to see her. This pleased the princess very much.

So the young man sat by her side and talked to her. He told her that her eyes were like beautiful dark lakes, in which thoughts swam about like little mermaids, and that her skin was like a soft plain. When he asked her if she would marry him, she agreed straight away.

"Come on Saturday," she said, "for my parents will be here for tea. How proud they will be when they find out I am going to marry an angel! But to win them over, you must think of a wonderful story to tell them, for they like stories better than anything."

"Very well," he replied, "I will bring them the gift of my very best tale." And so they parted.

When the 'angel' returned on Saturday, the king and queen received him with great politeness and curiosity.

"As you are an angel, you must have a wonderful story for us," remarked the king.

"Oh yes," said the queen, "please do tell us a tale."

"Certainly," the young man replied. "There was once a merchant's son," he began, "who had fallen on hard times. But luck soon came his way – he discovered a magical flying trunk. He soared away to a far-off country, where he met a beautiful princess. To gain her trust, he told her he was an angel.

"The princess was under a cruel enchantment that had taken away her wits and turned her into a fool – and not just her, but also her father and mother, the king and queen. However, the young man had heard many fairy stories on his travels and knew just how to break the spell –

obviously, he had to kiss the princess! The moment he had done so, the curse was lifted – the royal family were fools no more and could see everything clearly again.

"The princess married the merchant's son and of course, they all lived happily ever after," the young man finished, his fingers crossed hopefully behind his back.

"What an exciting story!" cried the king. "I really feel as if it had happened to me!"

"Yes, you certainly are a storyteller like no other!" agreed the queen. "You must marry our daughter and join our family! I can hardly wait for all the tales with which you are going to entertain us."

Only the princess sat still and silent, deep in thought.

The wedding day was fixed, and the evening before, a great festival was held in the city so everyone could celebrate. Coloured lanterns were lit, cakes and sweets were thrown among the people, and bands played music so everyone could dance in the streets. Altogether, it was a splendid affair.

'I will give everyone a treat of my own,' thought the merchant's son. So he took the four shillings, which was all the money he had left in the world, and went and bought

all sorts of fireworks. He packed them in his
trunk and flew up into the air.

What a tremendous show they made as
they went off! And how amazed everyone

was to see him flying around in the sky! The people really believed him to be an angel.

But alas, a spark from one of the fireworks landed on the flying trunk and set it alight. The merchant's son only just made it back down to the ground safely before the smouldering object burst into flames and burned away to ashes.

So the merchant's son could not fly any more, nor go to meet his bride. But perhaps that was just as well. The princess had realized that she had been tricked and was waiting to kick him out of the kingdom, for of course she didn't want to marry a liar – flying trunk or no flying trunk.

Today, the foolish merchant's son

wanders through the world making a living by telling fairytales – but none of them are as entertaining as his own story.

That's Not True!

A Hungarian fairytale retold by Baroness Orczy

Once upon a time there was a princess who was very beautiful – and also determinedly single. She did not want to marry any old prince or nobleman, so she thought up what she was sure was an impossible challenge for would-be suitors. The princess announced publicly that she would only marry the man who could tell her father, the king, a story that he could not believe.

That's Not True!

Of course, the whole point of being a gallant prince or a bold knight is that you are not put off by a challenge. So, to the princess's great dismay, noble suitors streamed to the castle from hundreds of miles around.

And what incredible stories they told! Many had travelled on brave quests across wide seas, through deep dark forests, over scorching deserts, up icy mountains that scraped the sky, and far into the depths of underground caverns. They told fantastic stories of the dragons and monsters they had fought, the witches and warlocks they had outwitted, the demons, dwarves and goblins they had tricked, and the curses and enchantments they had overcome.

But the king was old and had heard it all before. After all, he had been a young prince once and had gone out into the world to seek adventures and make his

name. He had faced much magic, many
perils and pestilences. Nothing was new to
him. Nothing was unbelievable.

So the flood of noble suitors gradually
dwindled to a stream, thinned to a trickle,
and then dried up altogether.

Now in a nearby village there dwelt a
poor young peasant called John, who had
heard about the princess's announcement.
One day, he summoned all his courage and
strode up to the king's castle. Although he
was trembling on the inside, he knocked
firmly at the gates and demanded an
audience with His Majesty.

The king knew very well what the
young fellow wanted. Even though John
wasn't noble, so many princes and knights

had come on the same errand and failed that the king was despairing that his daughter would ever marry. And what the king wanted most to cheer him in his old age was to hear the laughter of his grandchildren around the castle, and have them curl up on his lap as he sat on his throne, telling them his incredible stories. So the king gave the order for the young peasant to be admitted to the royal presence at once.

"Good morning, Your Majesty," John said, a little nervously.

"Good morning, my lad. Well, what do you want?" asked the king kindly.

"Please, Your Majesty, I have come as a suitor for your daughter."

"Very good," encouraged the king. "But I'm sorry to have to say it – you don't look as though you have a penny to your name. May I ask in what manner you would be able to keep her?"

"I dare say I could manage to keep her pretty comfortably indeed. My father owns a pig."

"Really?" said the king.

"A wonderful pig, Your Majesty," the lad went on. "This pig has kept my father, my mother, seven sisters, and myself, for the last twenty years."

"Indeed!" said the king, wondering how this was possible.

"He gives us as good a quart of milk every morning as any cow," said John.

"Indeed!" said the king, stroking his beard. "I suspect this is a magical pig then," he remarked.

"Yes sire, and he lays most delicious eggs for our breakfast," John remarked.

"Indeed!" said the king, scratching his head. "It must be a very strong magic," he said thoughtfully.

"And every day my mother cuts a nice bit of bacon out of his side, and every night it grows back again," John insisted.

"Indeed!" said the king, his eyes widening. "As I thought, an exceedingly strong and powerful magic."

"The other day the pig disappeared. My mother looked for him high and low, all over the village, but he was nowhere to

be seen," continued John.

"That must have been very sad," replied the king.

"Oh, it was, sire," agreed John. "But there was a happy ending. She finally found him in the larder, catching mice."

"Intelligent too – what a useful pig!" said the king, chuckling.

"He is exceedingly useful – my father sends him into town every day to do errands for him," John went on.

"How wise of your father," remarked the king.

"He ordered all of my father's clothes, and indeed mine too, from Your Majesty's own tailor."

"They do appear very well made!" said

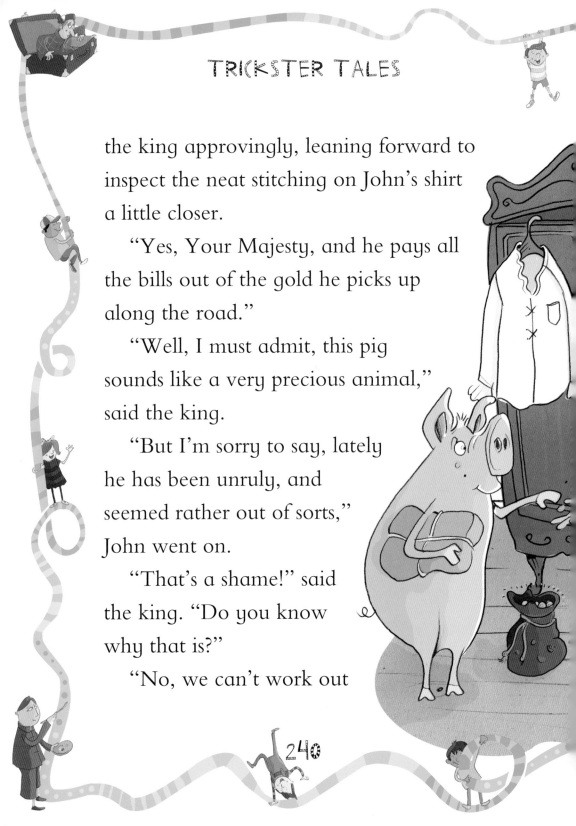

the king approvingly, leaning forward to inspect the neat stitching on John's shirt a little closer.

"Yes, Your Majesty, and he pays all the bills out of the gold he picks up along the road."

"Well, I must admit, this pig sounds like a very precious animal," said the king.

"But I'm sorry to say, lately he has been unruly, and seemed rather out of sorts," John went on.

"That's a shame!" said the king. "Do you know why that is?"

"No, we can't work out

the reason," sighed John. "He refuses to go where he is told, and won't allow my mother to have any more bacon from his side."

"Have you tried punishing him?" inquired the king, most intrigued.

"We can't bring ourselves to do that, Your Majesty," explained John. "We are so fond of the pig after all he has done for us, and we feel so sorry for him, as he is growing rather blind and can no longer see where he is going."

"What a shame! Yes, yes, you're right, of course. He should really be treated with the utmost kindness," agreed the king.

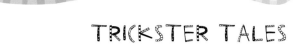

"Yes, Your Majesty, that is why my father has just engaged your father to be our pig-keeper," stated John.

"That's not true!" yelled the king, outraged at the peasant's unbelievably bold claim. Then suddenly he remembered his daughter's challenge…

So the king ordered the princess to marry the peasant. He never regretted it – and neither did she. For John was a most clever and amiable young man, and the princess soon fell deeply in love with him.

The couple lived happily in the castle with the king for very many years. They had several little sons and daughters who loved nothing better than to sit on the king's lap in his big throne while he told

them his incredible stories. And years later, when John became king himself, all his people declared they had never had so wise and witty a ruler.

The Fox and the Crow

Retold from an Aesop's fable

Once upon a time there lived a big black crow in a forest. One day she was perched on a branch, preening her sleek, glossy feathers and admiring herself in the stream below, when she spied a piece of cheese on the bank. She swooped down and picked up the tasty morsel in her beak. Then she flew back to the tree where she settled once more on a branch, the cheese held tightly in her beak so all her neighbours could see how clever and lucky she was.

Unbeknown to the crow, a wily fox was lurking in some bushes below. He saw what the crow had done and licked his lips at the thought of the delicious cheese. But how could he get it for himself? He needed to come up with a plan fast, before the crow grew tired of showing off the delicacy and ate it up.

Then all at once the fox had an idea. He strolled casually to the foot of the tree.

"Mistress Crow," he cried out, "how lovely you look today! How gleaming your feathers are, how sharp your beak and how wonderfully bright your eyes! I'm sure your voice must be just as beautiful. Do let me

245

hear it – please sing for me. Then I will go and tell everyone that you truly are the Queen of Birds."

Of course, the vain crow was thrilled by these words, and was more than happy to oblige. Without thinking, she lifted her head, tilted her beak proudly to the skies, and began to caw her coarse song. The cheese tumbled to the ground.

The gleeful fox pounced on it at once, snapping it up in his jaws. "Thank you, that was all I wanted," he said, swallowing the last morsel with a grin. "And in exchange for your most delicious cheese I will give you a piece of advice you would do well to remember in future – when people pay you compliments, they may not

The Fox and the Crow

always be telling the truth."

And the moral of the story is: do not trust flatterers.

Stan Bolovan

An Eastern European folk tale
told by Andrew Lang

A long time ago, a small, ramshackle house stood all alone on a moor. In the house lived a poor man named Stan Bolovan and his wife and their children – so many children that the couple had lost count of how many they had. Certainly too many for a poor man to feed.

There came a time when the family had eaten all the food in the house and there

was no money to buy more. Stan decided he must go out into the world to find some.

So Stan wandered and wandered and wandered till he reached the end of the world, and there he saw a shepherd with an enormous flock of sheep.

Stan waited till midnight and then crept up to the sheep, hoping he might steal some. But he was stopped in his tracks by a rushing noise, and through the air flew a big dragon, who swooped down and grabbed several sheep in his talons, before soaring off again. After this, Stan was too terrified to move.

The same thing happened the next night – and the next. And each morning, the shepherd moaned and groaned that he

could do nothing about it.

Stan thought of his hungry children at home and at last made himself known to the shepherd and said, "What will you give me if I rid you of the dragon?"

"Half of my flock, most willingly," answered the shepherd.

Stan thought of the fearsome dragon, but then he considered how long all those sheep would feed his starving children. "It's a deal," he replied firmly.

Just before midnight Stan positioned himself in the centre of the flock. Once again there was the sudden rush of air and the dragon came swooping down.

"Dear me!" exclaimed the dragon. "Who are you, small man, and where did

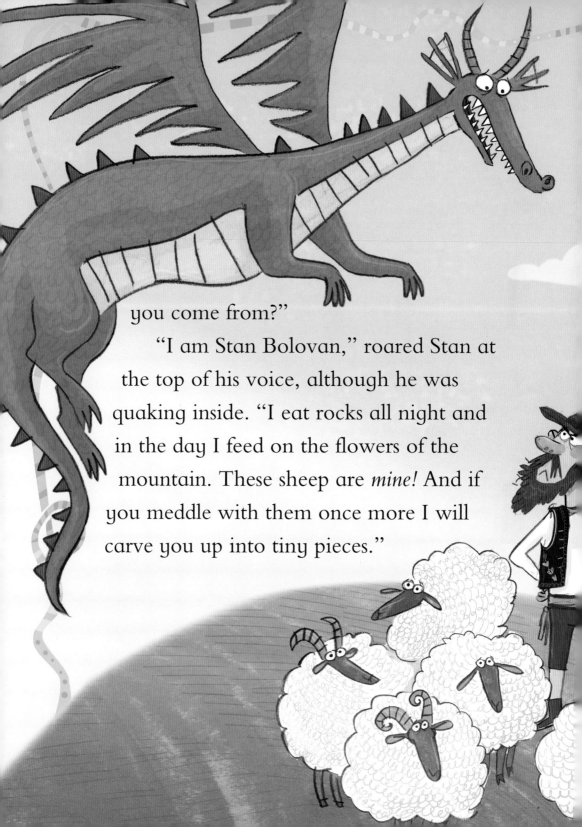

you come from?"

"I am Stan Bolovan," roared Stan at the top of his voice, although he was quaking inside. "I eat rocks all night and in the day I feed on the flowers of the mountain. These sheep are *mine!* And if you meddle with them once more I will carve you up into tiny pieces."

When the dragon heard these words he quailed, for no one had ever spoken to him like that before. He presumed that this Stan Bolovan must be a mighty hero, just like the ones he had heard about in all the old stories.

The fearful dragon thought quickly and came up with a plan to lure Stan home to where his mother was waiting, for she was bigger and much stronger than he. "Now don't be hasty," said the quaking dragon. "If you promise not to carve me into tiny pieces I will pay you seven sacks of gold coins. Come home with me now and I'll give them to you."

Seven sacks full of gold coins! Stan agreed at once,

and started along the road with the dragon.

The dragon's mother was as old as time itself. When she saw that her son had come home without any sheep she grew very angry and flames darted from her nostrils. But before she could speak, the dragon whispered in her ear: "Mother, this man eats rocks all night and in the day feasts on the flowers of the mountain. He carves dragons into tiny pieces! He's a proper hero, like in the old days."

"There is no need to be afraid," muttered the wise, old dragon in reply. "You did the right thing in bringing him here to me. We'll just wait until he is asleep. Then you take your club and hit him on the head. It is easily done."

And so it would have been if Stan hadn't outwitted them. That night, when the dragon and his mother had put out their lights, he stuffed an old sack with earth. Then he placed it in his bed and covered it with clothes, while he hid himself under the bed – just in case. He then began to snore very loudly.

Very soon the dragon came creeping into the room, and landed a tremendous blow on the spot where Stan's head should have been. Stan groaned loudly from under the bed, and, satisfied, the dragon stole away as softly as he had come.

Next morning, the dragon and his mother were having a slap-up breakfast when Stan came strolling down the stairs.

"Good morning," he said cheerily.

"G-g-g-good morning," stammered the dragon's mother, very surprised.

"How did you sleep?" the dragon inquired, totally baffled.

"Oh, very well thank you," replied Stan, casually rubbing his head, "but I dreamt that a flea had bitten me – in fact, I think one must have done, as I've got a tiny lump just here."

The dragon and his mother looked at each other in alarm. "Do you hear that?" the young dragon whispered.

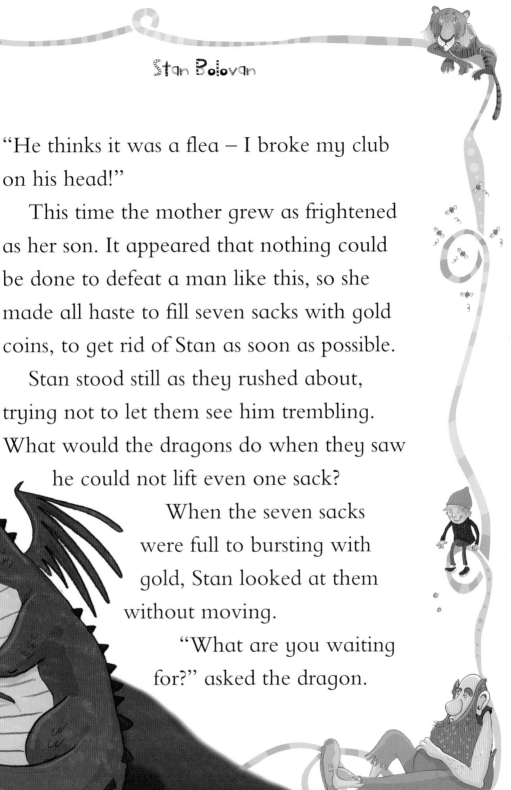

"He thinks it was a flea – I broke my club on his head!"

This time the mother grew as frightened as her son. It appeared that nothing could be done to defeat a man like this, so she made all haste to fill seven sacks with gold coins, to get rid of Stan as soon as possible.

Stan stood still as they rushed about, trying not to let them see him trembling. What would the dragons do when they saw he could not lift even one sack?

When the seven sacks were full to bursting with gold, Stan looked at them without moving.

"What are you waiting for?" asked the dragon.

"Well, do you know, I think I quite like it here," Stan sighed. "Do you mind if I stay a little longer?"

The mother dragon's face fell and her son gave a little shriek of dismay. "I'll tell you what," the mother dragon said, "let's make it eight sacks – and my son will carry them home for you himself." The words were hardly out of her mouth before the young dragon had snatched up the eight sacks of gold and piled them on his back. Then he and Stan set off.

They travelled and travelled, and at length Stan caught sight of his ramshackle

house and heard his children's voices. The boys and girls had had nothing to eat since Stan left, and they were starving. They came rushing towards him waving knives

and forks in their hands. At the sight of the dragon, they began to call out, "We will eat dragon's flesh, give us dragon's flesh!"

The dragon flung down the sacks in terror and flew away as fast as he could, back to the end of the world. And from that day to this, the dragons have never dared to show their faces again.

The Tiger, the Holy Man and the Jackal

An Indian folk tale retold by Joseph Jacobs

A tiger was once caught in a trap and then caged. He tried in vain to get out through the bars, and rolled and bit with rage and grief when he failed.

By chance a poor holy man came

walking by. "Have mercy on me and let me out of this cage, please, oh holy one!" cried the tiger.

"Nay, my friend," replied the holy man mildly, "for you would probably eat me if I did."

"Not at all!" swore the tiger with many oaths. "On the contrary, I should be forever grateful and serve you as a slave!"

As the tiger sobbed and sighed and wept in distress, the holy man's heart softened, and at last he consented to open the door of the cage. Out popped the tiger, and seizing the poor man, he cried out: "What a fool you are!

What is going to stop me from eating you now? For after being cooped up so long I am terribly hungry!"

The holy man begged and pleaded for his life, so the tiger summoned the few scraps of good nature he had, and decided instead to leave the matter in the hands of the universe. He told the holy man to ask three things whether they thought the tiger should eat him or not – and he promised to abide by their decision.

So the trembling holy man first asked a pipal tree what it thought of the matter. But the pipal tree replied coldly,

"What have you got to complain about? Think about me – I give shade and shelter to everyone who passes by, but do they show me gratitude? No, they do not! In return for my kindness they tear down my branches to feed their cattle. So don't ask me for sympathy – I have none for you!"

With great dismay in his heart, the holy man then walked through the countryside a little way till he came across a buffalo turning a well-wheel. But he fared the same with the buffalo, for it answered in a booming voice, "You are a fool to expect gratitude. Look at me! While I gave the people milk they fed me on cotton-seed and oil-cake, but now I am no longer good for milking they make me work all day in the

blazing sun, and give me nothing but rotting leftovers as fodder!"

The holy man then desperately asked the road to give him its opinion. "My dear sir," said the road, "how foolish you are to expect anything but greed! Here I am, useful to all, yet everyone – rich and poor, great and small – tramples on me as they travel along, throwing their rubbish at me as they go!"

At this, the holy man sorrowfully turned to make his way back to the tiger, as he had promised. On the way he met a jackal, who called out, "What's the matter, holy man? You look as miserable as a fish out of water!"

The holy man told him all that had

occurred. "How very confusing!" said the jackal, when the holy man had finished. "Would you mind telling me over again, for everything has got so mixed up!"

So the holy man told his tale all over again, but the jackal shook his head in a distracted sort of way.

"It's very odd," he said, "but I still don't understand! It all seems to go in one ear and out the other. If you take me to the place where it all happened then perhaps I shall be able to give a judgement."

So they returned to the cage where the tiger was waiting for the holy man, sharpening his teeth and claws.

"You've been away a long time!" growled the savage beast. "But now that

you have discovered how things really are in the world, let us begin our dinner."

'Our dinner!' thought the wretched holy man with a shudder of fear. 'What a remarkably delicate way of putting it!'

"Just give me five minutes, my lord," he pleaded, "in order that I may explain matters to the jackal here, who appears to be somewhat slow-witted."

The tiger consented and the holy man began the whole story over again, not missing a single detail and spinning as long a yarn as possible.

"Oh, my poor brain! Oh, my poor brain!" cried the jackal, wringing his paws in distress. "Let me see! How did it all begin? You were in the cage, and the tiger

came walking by—"

"Rot!" interrupted the tiger. "What a fool you are! *I* was in the cage."

"Of course!" cried the jackal, trembling with fright. "Yes! I was in the cage – no I wasn't. Dear, dear! Where are my wits? Let me see… the tiger was in the holy man, and the cage came walking by – no, that's not it, either! Well, don't mind me, but begin your dinner, for I shall never understand!"

"Yes, you shall!" returned the tiger, in a rage of frustration at the jackal's stupidity. "I'll make you understand! Look here – I am the tiger…"

"Yes, my lord!"

"And that is the holy man…"

"Yes, my lord!"

"And that is the cage…"

"Yes, my lord!"

"And I was in the cage – do you understand now?"

"Yes – no – please, my lord…"

"Well?" cried the tiger impatiently.

"Please, my lord, how did you get in?"

"How? In the usual way, of course!"

"Oh, dear me! My head is beginning to whirl again! Please don't be angry, my lord, but what is 'the usual way'?"

At this the tiger lost patience and, jumping into the cage, cried, "This way! Now do you understand how it was?"

"Perfectly!" grinned the jackal, as he swiftly slammed the door, revealing at once

his clever trick. "And if you will permit me to say so, I think matters should remain just as they were!"

Thor's Journey to the Land of the Giants

Adapted from a Norse myth told
by Charles John Tibbit

One day, Thor the thunder god set out
from Asgard, home of the gods, in his
great rumbling chariot drawn by two goats.
He took with him the god of mischief,

Loki, for company, and one servant – a human boy named Thjalfi.

They travelled far to the east, eventually entering Jotunheim, the land of the giants. There they journeyed all day through an immense forest until, finally emerging from the trees, they saw a city situated in the middle of a vast plain. They approached it in wonder.

The city wall was so lofty that you could not see the top of it without throwing your head back. When they reached the wall, they found the gateway closed with immense bars across it, which even Thor could not have broken apart. So he and his companions crept between them.

The travellers found themselves standing

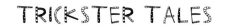

before a colossal palace. The door was
open, so they went in. They found
themselves in an enormous hall, filled with
hundreds of giant warriors. The giant in the
centre was clearly the king, Utgard-Loki,
whom they saluted with great respect.
However, he glanced at them and burst out

laughing. "If I'm not much mistaken," he boomed, "that little man there is the mighty thunder god, Thor!" And how all the giants laughed!

"I will give you a chance to prove that you are greater than your size," the giant king continued, to a roar of approval from his subjects. "Show us the best that you and your companions can do, and if you impress us, we promise we won't crush you – not today, at any rate."

Loki stepped forward without hesitation. "I can eat quicker than anyone else," he said, feeling confident (he was extremely hungry). "If there's anyone willing to compete with me, I will prove it."

So the king ordered one of his subjects,

Logi, to come forward, and try his skill against Loki. A great trough full of meat was placed in the hall. Loki positioned himself at one end and Logi set himself at the other. The two began to eat, gobbling through the meat and making quite a mess!

Presently they met in the middle of the trough, but Loki had only devoured the flesh of his portion, whereas the other had devoured both flesh and bones. All the company therefore decided that Loki had been beaten.

Then the boy Thjalfi declared that no man alive could beat him at running. So the king called forward a young giant named Hugi. "Ready… go!" he bellowed, and the two runners sped away. However,

Hugi ran so fast that he flashed around the enormous hall and returned to the starting-place while Thjalfi had hardly moved away from it. Then said the delighted king: "It's true, Thjalfi, that you are the fastest human I have ever seen, but you must run faster than that if you are to beat Hugi."

Utgard-Loki then turned to Thor and asked him in what manner he was going to prove himself. Thor threw out his chest and replied that he would contest the prize for the fastest drinker with anyone in the court. Utgard-Loki was mightily pleased and ordered his cup-bearer to bring out his drinking horn. It was massive, even by giant standards. The cup-bearer presented the immense drinking horn to Thor.

"The fastest drinker will empty that horn at a draught," said Utgard-Loki. "Some men make two draughts of it, but the most puny drinker will need three to empty it."

Thor put the horn to his mouth and, without drawing breath, drank as long and as deeply as he could, to avoid having to take a second draught. However, when he set the horn down and looked in it he could see that hardly any of the liquid was gone.

"You have drunk well," said Utgard-Loki, "but it is plain that you are not as mighty as you think. I will give you one last chance. The lads here play a game in which they lift my cat up. The one who lifts the cat the highest wins."

As he spoke, there sprang upon the hall floor an enormous grey cat. Thor went up to it, put his hand under its middle and tried to lift it from the floor. Thor strained and struggled, but when he had tried with all his might the cat had only one foot off the floor. "Enough!" bellowed the furious thunder god. "Someone come and fight me – then you'll truly

279

see how mighty I am!"

The giants all taunted and jeered as
Utgard-Loki called forward Elli, a toothless
old woman. Burning with humiliation,
Thor charged and grappled with her,
determined to lay her on the floor in a
second and then set to with the giant king
himself. But the harder Thor tightened his
hold, the firmer the old woman stood. To
Thor's horror, he felt himself totter. And at
last, after a long tussle, he fell to one knee.

King Utgard-Loki and the giants sprang
to their feet and, cheering with gusto,
ushered the travellers outside the city wall.

"Now I must tell you the truth,"
admitted the king, when at last the giants
had quietened. "Loki ate fast, but the name

'Logi' means 'flame' – he was eating against fire itself, which consumes everything. Thjalfi ran swiftly – but 'Hugi' means 'thought', which is the swiftest thing in the universe.

"The liquid in my drinking horn was in fact the mighty ocean. You drank so much of it that if I had not seen it with my own eyes, I should never have believed it. You did no less a wondrous thing when you lifted up the cat – which was a magical disguise for the immense Midgard serpent, which circles the world of men.

"Your wrestling match with Elli was, too, a great feat, for she is old age – and no one can defeat old age. Now I want you to leave my city – for now I know how

283

mighty you truly are, I shall never again allow you to enter it."

So Thor was forced to go on his way, never able to forget how he had been the subject of a giant-sized trick.

The Art Contest

A Vietnamese folk tale

Once upon a time – not that long ago – in Southeast Asia, there lived a boy called Trang Quynh. He was thirteen years old and he was the cleverest person in the country of Vietnam. He wasn't the cleverest person in the country of Vietnam by chance. Trang Quynh had worked very hard at it.

As soon as he started school, Trang Quynh had discovered that he really

enjoyed reading and he seemed to find remembering things much easier than the other children. He managed to learn all his times tables in just a week, and his classmates were so awed and his teacher so delighted that it spurred him on to memorize more. Soon he had learned the name of every insect and every type of plant in the rainforest, including all the details of their size, colour and medicinal uses.

Next, he learned the whole of *A History of Vietnam* until he could recite it off by heart. He was super-fast at working things out too. He could solve word and picture puzzles in only a second or two, calculate the most complex arithmetic as fast as a computer, and solve the most baffling brainteasers over just a cup of green tea.

It wasn't long before news began to spread of the boy with the super-brain. Day by day, curious neighbours and people from neighbouring towns and villages began to visit Trang Quynh's house, to challenge him with the hardest questions they could think of. Trang Quynh now had to study in the evening and late into the night, in order to continue learning all there was to learn and exercising his brain with new problems.

One day a woman asked him: "How long is the Mekong River?"

"Oh, that's an easy one," the boy replied. Without even having to think, he stated: "It's four thousand, three hundred and fifty kilometres." The boy looked at the woman expectantly. "Well, am I right?" he asked.

"I'm not sure," said the woman, embarrassed. "I don't know the answer myself." And she shuffled away in disgrace.

Up stepped a small child. "What is the capital city of Mexico?" he asked shyly.

"Ah, that's a trick question," Trang Quynh said, wagging his finger, although his eyes were shining with delight. "The capital city of Mexico is Mexico City."

The Art Contest

"You'll never guess this riddle," piped up a confident old man. "I have streets but no pavements, I have cities but no buildings, I have forests but no trees, I have rivers yet no water. What am I?"

"Oh, you'll have to do better than that," said Trang Quynh, laughing. "That's a map, of course." And the surrounding crowd clapped and *ooohed* and *aaahed* with wonder and delight.

"I have a big problem," announced a young farmer, "I cannot afford to pay workers to harvest my rice in the fields, so it rots before my family and I can gather all the crops. Can you invent a machine to help us?"

"Leave it with me overnight," said

Trang Quynh, and the next morning he presented the young farmer with a design for a harvesting machine that not only gathered rice twice as quick as any human could, but that also worked by clockwork, so it didn't cost anything to run.

Then one day, a man arrived in the village whom everybody knew to be a genius. He was famous for being an expert on many subjects and accomplished at many different skills. This man said to Trang Quynh, "I can make a drawing of not just one wild animal, but two – in only a minute." He picked up two paintbrushes, one in each hand, dipped them in a saucer of ink, and drew with just a few masterly strokes – *swish swish swish* – the most

amazing lion with his right hand and an incredible tiger with his left. "Now," the man said smugly to Trang Quynh, "can you, with your super-brain, top that?"

"Well, I'm not sure," said Trang Quynh, modestly, "but I will do my best." He spread out his ten fingers, dipped them in the ink, and drew them all down

the paper at the same time.

"Worms," he announced. "Ten wild animals in one second. I win."

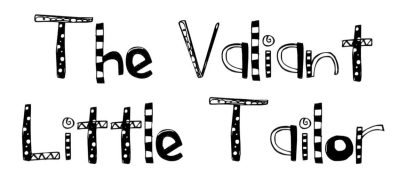

The Valiant Little Tailor

Adapted from a traditional tale
by the Brothers Grimm

There was once a little tailor who was a very cheeky chap. Maybe he was cheeky because he was little, I don't know. In any case, he was little and he was cheeky and he was a tailor – and that's the truth of it.

One day, the cheeky little tailor was sewing and nibbling on a thick slice of bread and jam (it was strawberry – his

favourite) when several big fat flies started buzzing round the jam jar. "Get lost!" he spluttered through a mouthful of crumbs. "Go away! Be off with you!" He flicked at the flies with his sewing, but the stubborn insects just buzzed round the jam jar more determinedly than ever. "I'll show you!" the tailor murmured, and he fetched his broom from the corner.

Very slowly (so as not to arouse the flies' suspicion), he lifted his broom high above his head and – *WHACK!* – brought it down swift and hard on the table. There was no more buzzing. When the cheeky little tailor lifted the broom and saw the seven dead flies underneath, his chest puffed up with pride. "Well, look at that!" he

crowed. "I've killed seven at one blow!
What a great hero I am!"

The tailor put aside his work, found
some silver material, and quickly ran
himself up a wide belt. He
decorated it with brightly
coloured beads and
embroidered it in

gold thread
with swirls and curlicues.
He then embroidered the
words: *seven at one blow*.

When it was finished, the tailor buckled the fine belt around his waist and stood in front of the mirror. "My, my!" he breathed. "What's a splendid champion like me doing in a dingy little workroom like this? I should be out and about in public, so everyone can admire me!"

With that, the cheeky little tailor left his house and set off down the road, humming merrily to himself and nodding politely to all he met.

Of course, everyone who bumped into the tailor along the road couldn't help but ask about the marvellous belt he wore. And the cheeky little tailor was only too delighted to explain that it was in honour of his slaying seven attackers with just one

294

blow of his weapon. He told himself it wasn't a lie, exactly. After all, he wasn't actually telling any untruths, he was just missing little bits out — that the seven attackers were actually flies and that his weapon of choice was a broom — and these were just minor details of no real interest to anyone anyway…

It wasn't long before everyone was gossiping about the hero who had killed seven at one blow. "Imagine slaying seven men at just one blow!" people exclaimed.

"No, it wasn't seven men," others insisted, "it was seven trolls!"

"You are wrong," others protested. "It wasn't seven trolls, it was seven dragons!"

Eventually, even the king got to hear of

the very small, but very brave, champion
and he asked him to the palace at once.
The tailor wasn't at all nervous – in fact he
was delighted!

He knocked on the enormous golden
gates and then strode through the mighty
marble halls with his head held high and a
confident swagger, as though he really
was the conquering hero that he
pictured himself to be. When the
cheeky little tailor reached the
throne room, he gave a low,
low bow and then stood
perfectly straight with his
chest puffed out, so
the king could clearly
see and admire the

bright, shimmering belt.

"You may rise," the king bade him graciously. "Whoops – I'm sorry, I didn't realize you already had." He gave an embarrassed little cough at his mistake.

"Welcome, mighty champion," he continued, still very surprised at the great hero's small stature. "I was hoping you could help me out with a problem." From his throne, the king looked the cheeky little tailor in the eye. "There are two giants who keep robbing my villages and killing my subjects. If you get rid of them, I'll give you half of my kingdom."

"And…" said the cheeky little tailor (because he was very cheeky like that).

"And what?" said the king, very puzzled.

"And your daughter's hand in marriage," chuckled the tailor. "It's only usual in cases like this."

"Oh very well," grumbled the king. "I'll give you my daughter's hand in marriage as well."

"Very well," chirped the tailor. "Two giants mean nothing to me. Don't forget that I have killed seven at one blow." And with a wink he strode off, his belt sparkling in the sunlight.

When the tailor found the giants, they were both fast asleep under a huge, shady oak tree. The tailor patted his belt comfortingly, picked up two large round pebbles, and tucked them into his shirt. Then he tried to creep up to the tree. He

had problems getting close, because each time he walked forward, the giants' enormous snores blew him back.

Finally, he made a mad run for it and – looking a little windswept – reached the trunk. He climbed nimbly into the branches and chuckled to himself. Then he took out one of the stones and dropped it, hitting the first sleeping giant – *plop!* – straight on the nose.

"Oi!" roared the giant, waking up at once and turning on his brother. "What did you do that for, dungbreath?"

"Do what?" mumbled the second giant, half-asleep.

"You know!" bellowed the first giant. "Don't do it again!" And he settled right

back down to sleep.

High up in the tree, the cheeky little tailor giggled and dropped his other stone. It bounced right off the first giant's nose.

"Oi!" he boomed, sitting bolt upright and glaring at his brother. "I told you not to do that, thunderpants!" And he socked the second giant right in the face.

"What on earth did you do that for, mouldybeard?" the wounded giant roared, and he punched his brother's arm.

That was the start of a giant fight that raged so long the people in the nearby village thought there was an earthquake. The cheeky little tailor was very nearly shaken out of the oak tree, but at the end of it, the giants both lay dead beneath him

and he had suffered nothing worse than a bruised bottom.

And that is how a tailor came to win half a kingdom and marry a princess – all through being a very cheeky chap. Maybe he was a cheeky chap because he was little, I don't know. In any case, he was little and he was cheeky and he was a tailor – and that's the truth of it.

The Never-ending Story

A traditional tale

Once upon a time, there was a village at the edge of a deep, dark forest. None of the villagers ever went into the forest, because they had heard that those who did never came out. No one knew what happened to them – they vanished without a trace. People often told spooky stories of ghosts that lurked in the heart of the forest, where the trees grew closest together and no sunlight could ever be seen. Others told

tales of an ogre – although it may have been a troll – that dwelt in a cave deep in the forest, where travellers' bones decorated the bushes. Some recited a famous poem about the black magic that enchanted the forest. Those who ventured in were cursed never to find their way out. They stumbled round and round in circles, growing more and more confused, until they dropped dead from thirst, starvation or exhaustion.

What no one knew, however, was that none of these tales was true. They had been made up long ago by the chief of a gang of robbers who had claimed a large

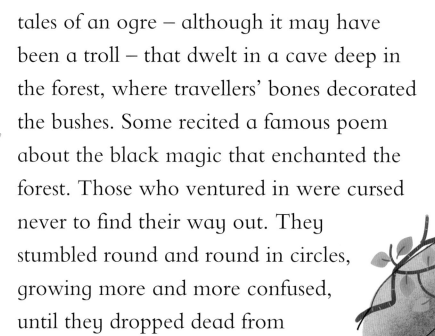

cavern in the forest as a hideout for his gang. He did not want villagers to come traipsing through the trees for a picnic and discover all his stolen gold, jewels and precious treasures. So he invented stories to trick everyone into staying well away.

The stories had done their work better than the robber chief could ever have imagined. And although he had grown old and passed away many years ago, his grandson – who was now the chief – was still never troubled by nosy

or bothersome villagers.

So the outlaws had become the most successful gang of bandits for miles around. They could plot and scheme in peace to their hearts' content. Once they had successfully raided, plundered and pillaged, they could disappear into the safety of the forbidden forest, and gloat over their ill-gotten gains without fear of discovery.

In fact, if the robber chief were to tell the truth for once (and he could not remember the last time that he had), he would have to admit that life had become rather dull. There were hardly any challenges for his gang any longer. There was little danger for them and so no accompanying sense of excitement. Something important was

missing from their lives – fun. The chief had begun to notice that his robbers had started to argue amongst themselves and fight more than usual – and over the smallest things. He could only put their irritability down to one thing – boredom.

So the chief thought up a cunning plan – a scheme to get his men's hearts pounding, pulses racing and blood pumping. He announced that every night, around the campfire, one of the robbers would tell the others a scary story – one which would strike fear into their hearts. And when the time came when they had each told their story, the robber who was voted to have told the scariest tale would win the enviable position of deputy robber chief.

They began that very night, as soon as they had eaten their dinner. The robber chief looked around at his men's expectant faces, flickering in the firelight. His little trick seemed to be working already – there was a definite shiver of excitement throughout the camp.

The chief's gaze came to rest on the meanest, ugliest one of them. "Bryan," he

said. "You have the honour of going first.
Start us off please – and make it scary!"

Bryan spat out of the corner of his
mouth, and said in a hoarse rasp: "Ok boss,
I will. Listen up all of you – and listen
good, or you'll feel the sting of my blade.
My story goes like this:

"Once upon a time, there was a village
at the edge of a deep, dark forest. None of
the villagers ever went in to the forest,
because they had heard that those who did
never came out. No one knew what
happened to them – they vanished without
a trace…"

Crazy Capers

A Mad Tea Party

Adapted from *Alice's Adventures in Wonderland*
by Lewis Carroll

There was a table set out under a tree in front of the house and the March Hare and the Hatter were having tea at it. A Dormouse was sitting between them, fast asleep, and the other two were using it as a cushion, resting their elbows on it, and talking over its head. The table was a large one, but the three were all crowded together at one corner of it. "No room! No room!" they cried out when they saw Alice coming.

"There's plenty of room!" said Alice indignantly, and she sat down in a large armchair.

"Have some wine," the March Hare said encouragingly.

Alice looked all round the table, but there was nothing on it but tea. "I don't see any wine," she remarked.

"There isn't any," said the March Hare.

"Then it wasn't very civil of you to offer it," said Alice angrily.

"It wasn't very civil of you to sit down without being invited," replied the March Hare sharply.

"I didn't know it was *your* table," said

Alice. "It's laid for a great many more than three."

The Hatter opened his eyes very wide at this, but all he said was, "Why is a raven like a writing-desk?"

'Come, we shall have some fun now!' thought Alice. 'I'm glad they've begun asking riddles.' "I believe I can guess that," she added aloud.

"Do you mean you think you can find out the answer to it?" said the March Hare.

"Exactly so," said Alice.

"Then you should say what you mean," the March Hare went on.

"I do," Alice hastily replied. "At least… I mean what I say – that's the same thing, you know."

"Not the same thing a bit!" said the Hatter. "You might just as well say that 'I see what I eat' is the same thing as 'I eat what I see'!"

"You might just as well say," added the March Hare, "that 'I like what I get' is the same thing as 'I get what I like'!"

"You might just as well say," added the Dormouse, who seemed to be talking in his sleep, "that 'I breathe when I sleep' is the same thing as 'I sleep when I breathe'!"

"It is the same thing with you," said the Hatter. Here the the party sat silent for a minute, while Alice thought over all she could remember about ravens and writing-desks, which wasn't much.

The Hatter was the first to break the

silence. "What day of the month is it?" he said, turning to Alice. He had taken his watch out of his pocket, and was looking at it uneasily, shaking it every now and then, and holding it to his ear.

"The fourth," Alice said.

"Two days wrong!" sighed the Hatter. "I told you butter wouldn't suit the works!" he added angrily to the March Hare.

"It was the best butter," the March Hare meekly replied.

"Some crumbs must have got in as well," the Hatter grumbled. "You shouldn't have put it in with the bread-knife."

The March Hare took the watch and looked at it gloomily. Then he dipped it into his cup of tea and looked at it again.

Alice had been looking over his shoulder with some curiosity. "What a funny watch!" she remarked. "It tells the day of the month and not what o'clock it is!"

"Why should it?" muttered the Hatter. "Does your watch tell you what year it is?"

"Of course not," Alice replied very readily. "But that's because it stays the same year for such a long time together."

"Which is just the case with mine," said the Hatter. Alice felt dreadfully puzzled.

"Have you guessed the riddle yet?" the Hatter said.

"No, I give it up," Alice replied. "What's the answer?"

"I haven't a clue," said the Hatter.

"Nor I," said the March Hare.

Alice sighed wearily. "I think you might do something better with the time," she said, "than waste it in asking riddles that have no answers."

"If you knew Time as well as I do," said the Hatter, "you wouldn't talk about wasting *it*. It's *him*."

"I don't know what you mean," Alice cautiously replied.

"Of course you don't!" the Hatter said, tossing his head. "I dare say you never even spoke to Time! I last saw him in March, at the great concert given by the Queen of Hearts. I had to sing:

'Twinkle, twinkle, little bat!
How I wonder what you're at!

Up above the world you fly,
Like a tea-tray in the sky.
Twinkle, twinkle…'"

Here the Dormouse began singing in his sleep, "Twinkle, twinkle, twinkle, twinkle…" and went on so long that they had to pinch him to make him stop.

"Well, I'd hardly finished the first verse," said the Hatter, "when the Queen bawled, 'He's murdering Time! Off with his head!' Ever since, he won't do a thing I ask! It's always six o'clock now."

An idea came to Alice. "Is that why so many tea-things are put out here?" she asked.

"Yes," said the Hatter with a sigh. "It's

always tea-time and we've no time to wash the things between whiles."

"Then you keep moving round, I suppose?" said Alice.

"Exactly, as things get used up."

"I'm getting tired of this," the March Hare interrupted, yawning. "I vote the Dormouse tells us a story."

"Wake up, Dormouse!" they both cried.

The Dormouse slowly opened his eyes. "I wasn't asleep," he said feebly. "I heard every word you fellows were saying."

"Tell us a story!" said the March Hare.

"And be quick," added the Hatter, "or you'll be asleep again before it's done."

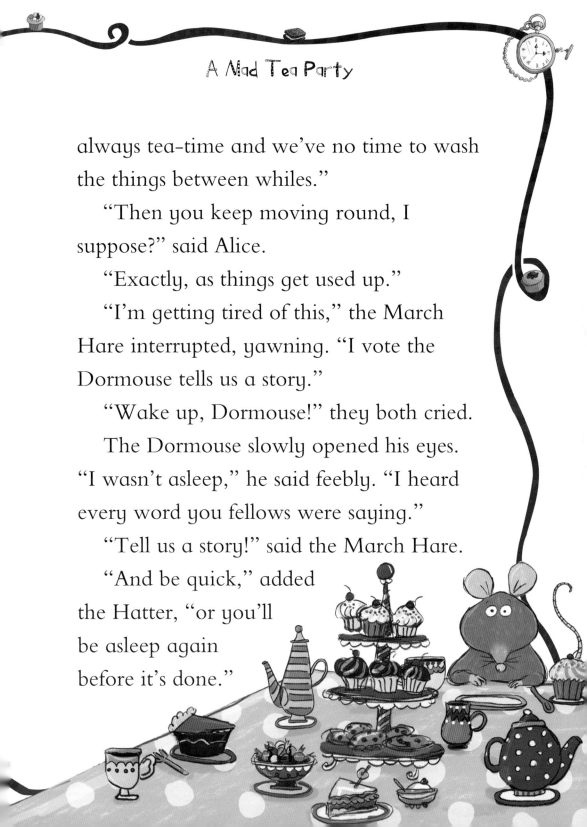

"There were once three little sisters," the Dormouse began in a great hurry. "Their names were Elsie, Lacie and Tillie, and they lived at the bottom of a well…"

"What did they live on?" said Alice.

"They lived on treacle," said the Dormouse, after thinking a minute or two. "It was a treacle-well."

"There's no such thing!" Alice cried.

The Dormouse sulkily remarked, "Finish the story yourself."

"No, please go on!" Alice said very humbly, "I won't interrupt again."

So the Dormouse went on, yawning and rubbing his eyes. "These three little sisters — they were learning to draw…"

"What did they draw?" said Alice, quite

forgetting her promise.

"Treacle," said the Dormouse, without considering at all this time.

"I want a clean cup," interrupted the Hatter. "Let's all move one place on."

He moved on as he spoke, and the Dormouse followed him. The March Hare moved into the Dormouse's place, and Alice rather unwillingly took the place of the March Hare. The Hatter was the only one who got any advantage from the change, and Alice was a good deal worse off than before, as the March Hare had just upset the milk-jug into his plate.

Alice did not wish to offend the Dormouse again, so said very cautiously, "But I don't understand… "

"Well then you shouldn't talk," the Hatter declared.

This rudeness was more than Alice could bear. She got up in disgust and walked off. The Dormouse fell asleep instantly, and neither of the others took the least notice of her going, though she looked back once or twice, half hoping they would call after her. The last time she saw them, they were trying to put the Dormouse into the teapot.

"At any rate I'll never go *there* again!" said Alice as she picked her way through the wood. "It's the stupidest tea party I ever was at in all my life!"

Lazy Jack

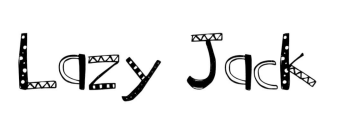

Adapted from a traditional tale told
by Joseph Jacobs

There was once a young man whose name was Jack, and he lived with his mother on a common. They were very poor. Jack's mother earned a living by spinning, but Jack was lazy and he did nothing but bask in the sun in hot weather and sit by the fire in winter-time. So people called him Lazy Jack. His mother could not get him to do anything for her.

Eventually, one Monday she could stand it no longer. She told him that if he did not begin to work for his porridge, she would have to turn him out to fend for himself.

This brought Jack to his senses, and the very next day he hired himself to a farmer for a penny. He laboured all day for his money, but as he was coming home, he lost his hard-earned coin while passing over a brook. "You stupid boy," said his mother, "you should have put it in your pocket."

"I'll do so next time," replied Jack.

On Wednesday, Jack went out again and hired himself to a cowherd, who gave him a jug of milk for his work. Jack took the jug and put it into the large pocket of his jacket, spilling it all before he got home.

"Dear me," said his old mother. "You should have carried it in your hands."

"I'll do so next time," replied Jack.

On Thursday Jack hired himself to a cheese-maker, who agreed to give him a cream cheese for his services. In the evening Jack took the cheese, and went home clutching it tight in his hands. By the time he got home the cream cheese had all melted and was dripping between his fingers. "You stupid boy," said his mother, "you should have carried it in a bag."

"I'll do so next time," replied Jack.

On Friday, Jack again went

out and hired himself to a baker, who gave
him a large cat for his work. Jack thrust the
cat into a bag, threw it over his shoulder,
and began striding home. But the furious
animal fought so hard to get out of the bag
that Jack's back was soon scratched to
ribbons, and he was forced to let it go.

When Jack got home, his mother said
to him, "You silly fellow, you should have
tied a string around its neck and led it
along after you."

"I'll do so next time," replied Jack.

On Saturday, Jack hired himself to a
butcher, who rewarded him with the
handsome present of a shoulder of mutton.
Jack took the mutton, tied a string around
it, and trailed it along after him in the dirt,

so that by the time he had got home the meat was completely spoiled. His mother was by this time quite out of patience with him, for the next day was Sunday, and now they were going to have to make do with just cabbage for their dinner.

"You ninney-hammer," she said, "you should have carried it on your shoulder."

"I'll do so next time," replied Jack.

On the following Monday Jack hired himself to a shepherd, who gave him a donkey for his trouble. Jack found it difficult to hoist the donkey onto his shoulders, but at last he did it, and began walking slowly home with his prize.

Now it happened that in the course of his journey he went past the house of a rich

man, who lived there with his daughter. She was a beautiful girl, but could not hear or speak. She had never laughed in her life, and the doctors said she would never speak till somebody made her laugh.

This young lady happened to be looking out of the window when Jack was passing with the donkey on his shoulders, its legs sticking up in the air. The sight was so comical and strange that she burst out into a great fit of laughter – and immediately recovered her speech and

hearing. Her father was
overjoyed, and immediately
ushered Jack in and offered
the girl's hand in marriage.
Thus Lazy Jack
became a rich man, and
he and his wife were
very happy. They had
a big house, and
Jack's mother
lived with them
in great happiness
until she died.

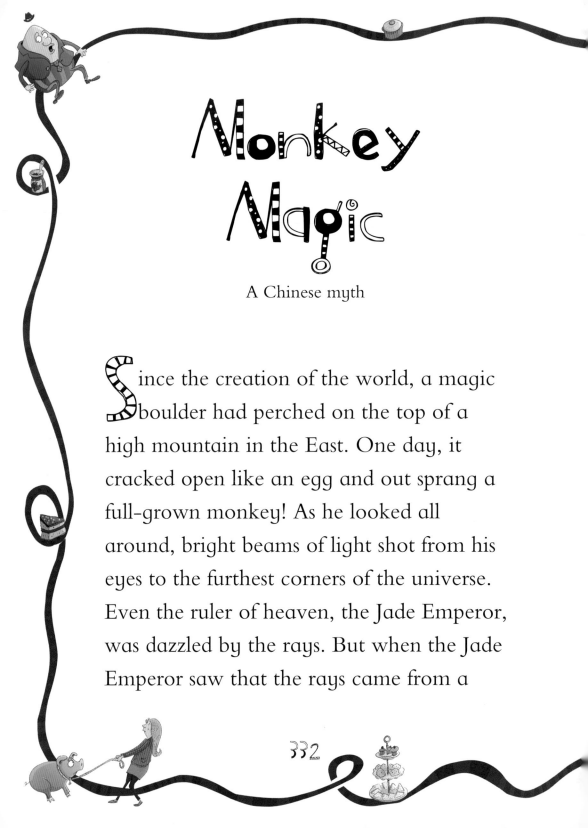

Monkey Magic

A Chinese myth

Since the creation of the world, a magic boulder had perched on the top of a high mountain in the East. One day, it cracked open like an egg and out sprang a full-grown monkey! As he looked all around, bright beams of light shot from his eyes to the furthest corners of the universe. Even the ruler of heaven, the Jade Emperor, was dazzled by the rays. But when the Jade Emperor saw that the rays came from a

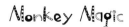

monkey, he sighed with great relief. "It's only a monkey," he said to himself. "How much mischief can one monkey make?"

If only the Jade Emperor had known!

The monkey was bold and daring, and quickly became king of all the monkeys. After four hundred years, he set his sights higher – he wanted to become immortal, or better still, one of the gods in heaven.

Through many years of hard study, Monkey acquired magic arts. He learned how to change into anything he wanted, to summon a cloud and ride upon it, and – most importantly – the secret of eternal life.

Then, Monkey visited the Dragon King and begged for a magic weapon that befitted his new immortal status. The

CRAZY CAPERS

Dragon King didn't dare say no to such a powerful creature. He gave Monkey a lethal iron staff, which could shrink to the size of a needle so Monkey could keep it safely in his ear.

Not long afterwards, up in heaven, the Jade Emperor heard a commotion outside the East Gate. His chief minister hurried up to him in a fluster. "Your Imperial Highness, a talking monkey is clamouring to be let into heaven and become a god. He says he knows magic and is immortal – and I'm inclined to believe him, as he's just fought off four guards with an iron staff!"

"Indeed," said the Jade Emperor, stroking his long beard. He thought for a moment and then said: "Well, maybe the way to stop this monkey causing trouble is not through force but through wit. Invite him in and offer him a job. That way, we can keep an eye on him and make sure he doesn't go creating havoc."

So the chief minister hurried back to Monkey

and offered him the position of Supervisor of the Imperial Stables and Protector of the Imperial Horses.

"What an important role!" Monkey exclaimed, very pleased.

However, his delight didn't last long. He soon discovered that the job consisted largely of mucking out the stables – Monkey spent most of every day knee-deep in dung.

When he realized he had been tricked, he jumped up and down with rage. "So this is what the gods think of me, is it?" he screeched. "Me? The immortal Monkey King? Well, I won't stand for it!"

He rushed out of the stables, somersaulted onto a cloud, and sped off to

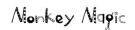

confront the Jade Emperor.

"Oh magical Monkey," the Jade Emperor soothed, "I apologize if my chief minister offended you. I meant for him to offer you a different position – the Invincible Peerless Guardian of the Garden of the Peaches of Immortality."

"Is that an important job?" the suspicious monkey asked gruffly. "Really?"

"Oh yes, really. Highly important," assured the Jade Emperor.

So Monkey accepted it.

Every day, Monkey stood at the gateway to the Garden of the Peaches of Immortality and kept watch for intruders, his iron staff at the ready. He watched… and watched… and watched… but no one

ever came. Nothing ever happened.
Monkey just stood there watching the grass
and the flowers and the immortal peach
trees grow, day after day. How utterly
boring it was! After a while, he realized
that he had once again been duped. The
Jade Emperor was just keeping him out of
everyone's way.

"I'll show him what I think of his stupid
peaches!" Monkey raged. He charged into
the garden, tore down the Peaches of
Immortality and ate every last one.
Monkey gorged himself until he felt sick,
and so he had to lie down and sleep it off.

While he was sleeping, the Jade Emperor
came riding up in a chariot to inspect his
sacred peaches. He was aghast at what he

saw. "That fiendish monkey!" he cried. "What am I to do with him?"

There was only one thing for it. The Jade Emperor sent a message to the Western Paradise, asking the assistance of the Buddha.

So Monkey woke from his stupor to find a huge man wearing a robe, hovering in front of him on a magic cloud.

"Who are you?" cried Monkey rudely.

The man just laughed. "I am the Buddha. I understand you want a high position in heaven."

"Of course!" stated the arrogant monkey. "I have great powers. I have mastered the arts of transformation, cloud-soaring and immortality."

"Indeed," smiled the Buddha. "Well, I am here to teach you the art of humility."

Monkey shrugged. He wasn't sure what 'humility' meant.

"I'll make you a bet," the Buddha said calmly. "If you can jump out of the palm of my hand, the Jade Emperor's throne is yours. But if you cannot, you will return to Earth immediately."

Monkey threw back his head and laughed. "You're on," he said. He shrunk his iron staff and tucked it in his ear, and jumped onto the Buddha's palm. Then he leapt with all his might.

Monkey sped through the air like a bolt of lightning for thousands of miles, until he landed in a place where five olive-coloured pillars reached up into the sky. "This must be the very edge of heaven," he told himself. As proof he had been there, he wrote on the foot of one of the pillars: "Here was Monkey." Then he leapt through the air and landed back in the

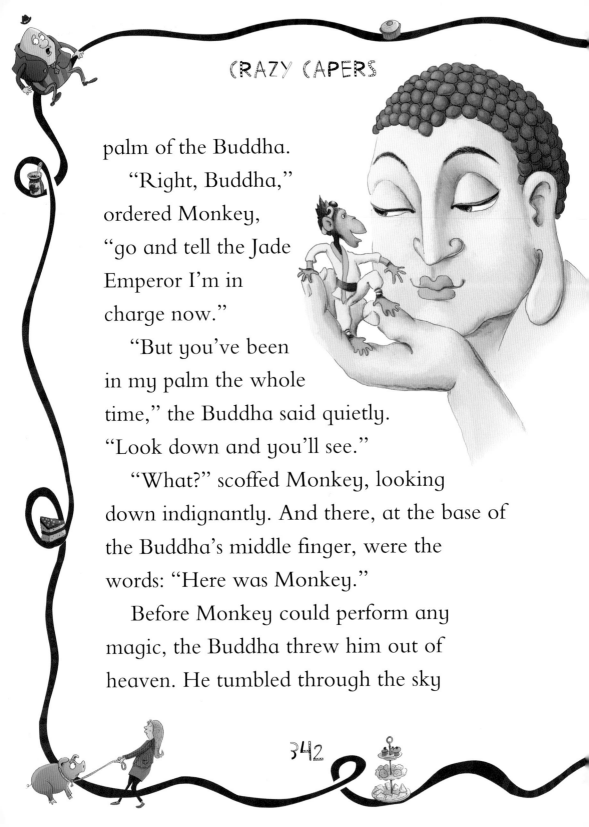

palm of the Buddha.

"Right, Buddha,"
ordered Monkey,
"go and tell the Jade
Emperor I'm in
charge now."

"But you've been
in my palm the whole
time," the Buddha said quietly.
"Look down and you'll see."

"What?" scoffed Monkey, looking
down indignantly. And there, at the base of
the Buddha's middle finger, were the
words: "Here was Monkey."

Before Monkey could perform any
magic, the Buddha threw him out of
heaven. He tumbled through the sky

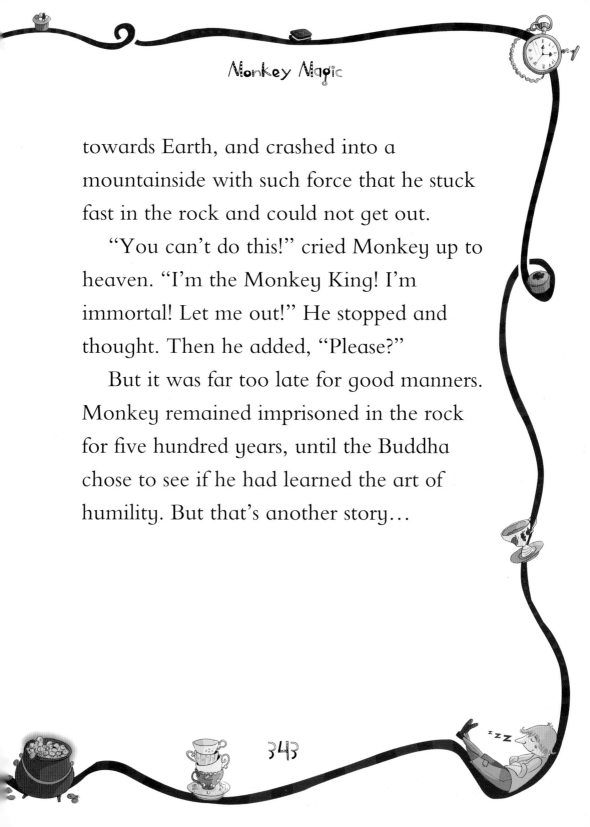

towards Earth, and crashed into a mountainside with such force that he stuck fast in the rock and could not get out.

"You can't do this!" cried Monkey up to heaven. "I'm the Monkey King! I'm immortal! Let me out!" He stopped and thought. Then he added, "Please?"

But it was far too late for good manners. Monkey remained imprisoned in the rock for five hundred years, until the Buddha chose to see if he had learned the art of humility. But that's another story…

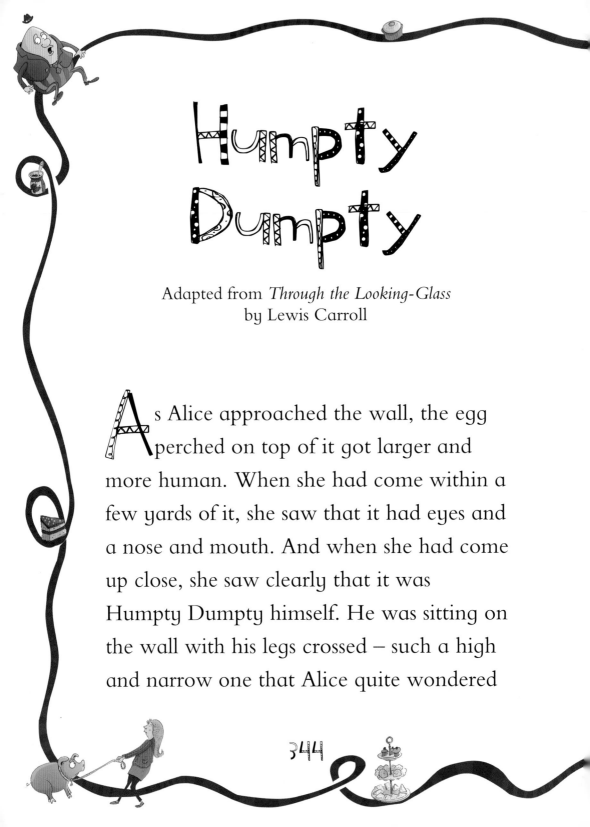

Humpty Dumpty

Adapted from *Through the Looking-Glass*
by Lewis Carroll

As Alice approached the wall, the egg perched on top of it got larger and more human. When she had come within a few yards of it, she saw that it had eyes and a nose and mouth. And when she had come up close, she saw clearly that it was Humpty Dumpty himself. He was sitting on the wall with his legs crossed – such a high and narrow one that Alice quite wondered how he could keep his balance.

"How exactly like an egg he is!" she said, standing with her hands ready to catch him, for she was every moment expecting him to fall.

"It's *very* provoking," Humpty Dumpty said, looking away from Alice as he spoke, "to be called an egg – *very*!"

"I said you *looked* like an egg, sir," Alice gently explained.

"Some people," said Humpty Dumpty, "have no more sense than a baby!"

Alice didn't know what to say to this. It wasn't at all like a conversation, as he never said anything to her. In fact, his last remark was evidently addressed to a tree. So she stood and softly repeated to herself:

"'Humpty Dumpty sat on a wall,
Humpty Dumpty had a great fall.
All the King's horses and all the King's men
Couldn't put Humpty Dumpty in his
place again.'

"That last line is much too long for the
poetry," she added.

"Don't stand there chattering to yourself
like that," Humpty Dumpty said, looking
at her for the first time. "Tell me your
name and your business."

"My name is Alice, but—"

"It's a stupid enough name!" Humpty
Dumpty interrupted impatiently. "What
does it mean?"

"*Must* a name mean something?" Alice

asked doubtfully.

"Of course it must," Humpty Dumpty said with a laugh. "*My* name means the shape I am. With a name like yours, you might be any shape, almost."

"Why do you sit out here all alone?" said Alice, wishing to avoid an argument.

"Why, because there's nobody with me!" cried Humpty Dumpty.

"Don't you think you'd be safer down on the ground?" Alice went on. "That wall is so very narrow!"

"Of course I don't think so!" growled Humpty Dumpty. "Why, if ever I *did* fall off – which there's no chance of – but if I did, the *King* has promised me to—"

"Send all his horses and all his men,"

347

Alice interrupted, rather unwisely.

"Now I declare that's too bad!" Humpty Dumpty cried, breaking into a sudden passion. "You've been listening at doors – and behind trees – and down chimneys – or you couldn't have known it!"

"I haven't, indeed!" Alice said very gently. "It's in a book."

"Ah, well! They may write such things in a *book*," Humpty Dumpty said in a calmer tone. "That's what you call a history of England, that is. However, this conversation is going on a little too fast. Let's go back to the last remark but one."

"I'm afraid I can't quite remember it," Alice said very politely.

"In that case we start fresh," said

Humpty Dumpty. "It's your turn to choose a subject…"

"Would you kindly tell me the meaning of the poem called *Jabberwocky*?" said Alice.

"Let's hear it," said Humpty Dumpty. "I can explain all the poems that were ever invented – and a good many that haven't been invented just yet."

This sounded very hopeful, so Alice repeated the first verse:

> ""'Twas brillig, and the slithy toves
> Did gyre and gimble in the wabe,
> All mimsy were the borogoves,
> And the mome raths outgrabe.'"

"That's enough to begin with," Humpty

Dumpty interrupted. "There are plenty of hard words there. 'Brillig' means four o'clock in the afternoon – the time when you begin broiling things for dinner."

"And what about 'slithy'?" said Alice.

"Well, 'slithy' means 'lithe and slimy'. 'Lithe' is the same as 'active'. You see, there are two meanings packed up into one word."

"I see it now," Alice remarked thoughtfully. "And what are 'toves'?"

"Well, 'toves' are something like badgers – they're something like lizards – and they're something like corkscrews."

"They must be very curious creatures."

"They are that," said Humpty Dumpty.

"And what's the 'gyre' and to 'gimble'?"

"To 'gyre' is to go round and round like a gyroscope. To 'gimble' is to make holes like a gimlet."

"And 'the wabe' is the grass-plot round a sundial, I suppose?" said Alice, surprised at her own ingenuity.

"Of course it is. It's called 'wabe', you know, because it goes a long way before it and a long way behind it—"

"And a long way beyond it on each side," Alice added.

"Exactly so. Well, then, 'mimsy' is 'flimsy and miserable'. And a 'borogove' is a thin, shabby-looking bird with its feathers sticking out all round – like a live mop."

"And then 'mome raths'?" said Alice. "I'm afraid I'm giving you a lot of trouble."

"Well, a 'rath' is a sort of green pig. But 'mome' I'm not certain about. I think it's short for 'from home' – meaning that they'd lost their way, you know."

"And what does 'outgrabe' mean?"

"Well, 'outgrabing' is something between bellowing and whistling, with a sneeze in the middle. You'll hear it done, maybe – down in the wood yonder – and once you've heard it you'll be *quite* content. Who's been repeating all that stuff to you?"

"I read it in a book," replied Alice.

"That's all," said Humpty Dumpty. "Goodbye."

'This was sudden,' Alice thought, but, after such a strong hint that she ought to be going, she felt that it would hardly be civil

355

to stay. "Goodbye!" she said cheerfully.

Alice waited to see if he would speak again, but as he didn't take further notice of her, she walked away. She couldn't help saying to herself as she went, "Of all the unsatisfactory people I *ever met*—" She never finished the sentence, for at this moment a heavy crash shook the forest from end to end.

"Oh dear," sighed Alice.

The Old Woman and the Crooked Sixpence

A traditional tale told by Charles John Tibbits

An old woman was sweeping her house when she found a crooked sixpence. "What shall I do

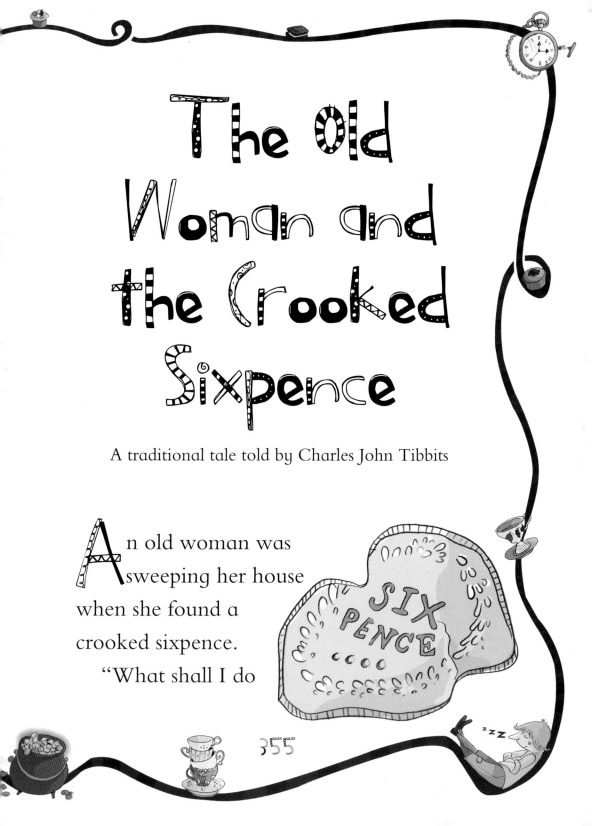

355

with this sixpence?" she said. "I will go to the market and buy a pig with it."

She went, and as she was coming home she came to a stile. Now the pig would not go over the stile. So the woman went on a little further and met a dog.

"Dog," she said, "bite pig. Piggy won't go over the stile, and I shan't get home tonight."

But the dog would not bite the pig. So the woman went on a little further and met a stick.

"Stick," she said, "beat dog. Dog won't bite pig, piggy won't go over the stile, and I shan't get home tonight."

But the stick would not. So the woman went on a little further and met a fire.

"Fire," she said, "burn stick. Stick won't beat dog, dog won't bite pig, piggy won't go over the stile, and I shan't get home tonight."

But the fire would not. So the woman went on a little further, and she met some water.

"Water," she said, "quench fire. Fire won't burn stick, stick won't beat dog, dog won't bite pig, piggy won't go over the stile, and I shan't get home tonight."

But the water would not. So the woman went on a little further and met an ox.

"Ox," she said, "drink water. Water won't quench fire, fire won't burn stick, stick won't beat dog, dog won't bite pig, piggy won't go over the stile, and I shan't

get home tonight."

But the ox would not. So the woman went on again, and met a butcher.

"Butcher," she said, "kill ox. Ox won't drink water, water won't quench fire, fire won't burn stick, stick won't beat dog, dog won't bite pig, piggy won't go over the stile, and I shan't get home tonight."

But the butcher would not. The woman went on a little further and met a rope.

"Rope," she said, "hang butcher. Butcher won't kill ox, ox won't drink water, water won't quench fire, fire won't burn stick, stick won't beat dog, dog won't bite pig, piggy won't go over the stile, and I shan't get home tonight."

But the rope would not. Again the

woman went on, and she met a rat.

"Rat," she said, "gnaw rope. Rope won't hang butcher, butcher won't kill ox, ox won't drink water, water won't quench fire, fire won't burn stick, stick won't beat dog, dog won't bite pig, piggy won't go over the stile, and I shan't get home tonight."

But the rat would not. The woman went on a little further and met a cat.

"Cat," she said, "kill rat. Rat won't gnaw rope, rope won't hang butcher, butcher won't kill ox, ox won't drink water, water won't quench fire, fire won't burn stick, stick won't beat dog, dog won't bite pig, piggy won't go over the stile, and I shan't get home tonight."

"Oh," said the cat. "I will kill the rat if you will fetch me some milk from that cow over there."

So the old woman went to the cow and asked her to let her have some milk for the cat.

"No," said the cow, "I won't let you have any milk unless you bring me some hay from that stack over there."

Away went the old woman to the stack and fetched the hay and gave it to the cow. Then the cow gave her some milk, and the old woman took it to the cat.

When the cat had lapped the milk, the cat began to kill the rat, the rat began to gnaw the rope, the rope began to hang the butcher, the butcher began to kill the ox, the ox began to drink the water, the water began to quench the fire, the fire began to burn the stick, the stick began to beat the dog, the dog began to bite the pig, and piggy, in a fright, jumped over the stile. So the old woman got safely home that night.

A Tall Tale

A North American folk tale

"What a big baby!" folk would say to Mrs Bunyan as they peered into the crib at her baby. "He's going to grow up to be a big lad, isn't he?"

But no one could have guessed how fast her son would grow, or how big. After just a week, little Paul was not so little at all and had to wear teenage-sized clothes. His infant lungs were so strong that, when he cried, his wails were so loud he scared all the creatures out of the pond two miles down the lane. After only two weeks, milk would no longer satisfy him. Mrs Bunyan had to give her baby forty bowls of porridge at each feed!

By the time Paul had reached school age, he was bigger and stronger than all the men in town. One morning, the townsfolk were roused from their slumbers by an almighty *BANG!* and the sound of shattering glass. They ran out into the street in their nightclothes, most alarmed, to be greeted by Paul's father waving his hands and crying out: "Don't panic! There's no problem! Paul has just got a slight cold – he sneezed and our windows blew out."

No one grumbled about little accidents such as this, as despite his immense height and strength, Paul was a very gentle, likeable fellow. Still, he did find it difficult to make friends with other children, as he was too big to join in with their games. For instance, there's no point in playing tag when your arms and legs are so long that you can reach the other children without even having to run. And making a den in the woods is no fun when you can't fit in it.

So on his tenth birthday, Mr Bunyan bought Paul a pet to keep him company.

And just as Paul was an extraordinary boy, his pet was an extraordinary pet – a bright blue ox named Babe.

From the moment Paul was given Babe they were inseparable and went everywhere together. And no one was all that surprised when Babe grew giant-sized himself. He was so big that a whole barn was needed to house him. It might have been some strange effect that rubbed off on the ox from always being with Paul, or it might have been that Babe was just naturally enormous

like his owner – no one was ever sure, but
no one was ever bothered either.

Mr and Mrs Bunyan did worry from
time to time about what Paul would do to
make a living. But they needn't have been
concerned. When he grew up, Paul found
himself the perfect job as a lumberjack.
Now, lumberjacks cut down trees for wood
– and in those days wood was used a great
deal: to build new homes and make
furniture for those homes, to build shops
and hotels and churches and jails, to make
wagons to carry people and goods, to make
sleepers for train tracks, and to make
telegraph poles.

Paul set up the biggest and best logging
camp in all of North America. He worked

with seven other lumberjacks, all over
six feet tall, and all called Elmer – so when
he called, they all came running. He hired
two chefs to cook them pancakes on
griddles so huge that they could only grease
them by strapping hams on their feet and
skating around them. And he filled the lake
behind his camp with bubbling pea soup.
This way, Paul made sure that his workers
were never hungry.

    With his team, Paul felled so many trees
that in just one week his book-keeper used
up more than twenty barrels of ink in
recording them all. Paul also fixed the end
of the winding road to the logging camp
onto Babe's harness, and got the mighty ox
to heave and drag the road out straight, so

the logs could be taken away more easily.

It's all true, I tell you – no word of a lie! But what most folk say is Paul Bunyan's greatest feat is when he was too tired to pick up his axe as he walked home one evening. By leaving it trailing along the ground as he walked, he carved an enormous cleft in the ground – today known as the Grand Canyon.

So you could say that Paul Bunyan even helped to shape North America.

The First Moccasins

A Native American traditional tale

Long ago, a tribe on the Great Plains had a mighty warrior chief. But he had one weakness – extremely sore feet. All the tribespeople went barefoot, running swift as hares through the long grasses. But none of them suffered with sore feet like the chief. His feet were always red and rubbed raw, with torn and tattered toenails. The chief knew that other tribes laughed at him behind his back. And when he caught some

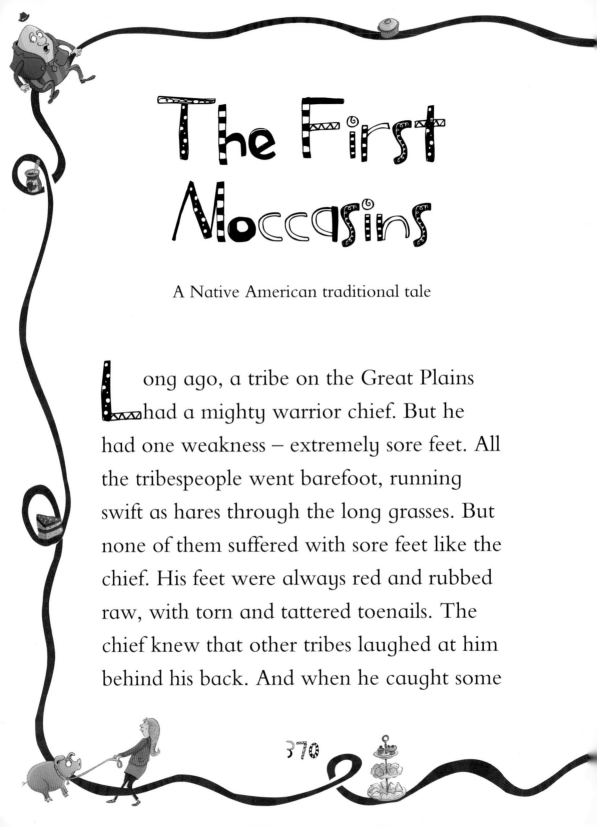

of the children in his own tribe pointing
and sniggering, he'd had enough! He
ordered his medicine man to find an answer
– or else.

The fearful medicine man thought of a
plan. He commanded the tribeswomen to
gather lots of reeds, and with them weave a
long, narrow mat. Then he appointed four
braves to roll the mat out in front of the
chief whenever he wanted to go anywhere,
so he could walk on it.

When the medicine man demonstrated
his idea, the chief grunted, "Humph!" and
hid a smile.

It worked reasonably well for a while.
But whenever the length of mat ran out,
and the chief had to wait for the four

braves to gather it up and roll it out again, it annoyed him immensely. One day, he grew so frustrated at standing there helplessly while the braves scurried round him that he roared: "This is ridiculous! I want the whole earth covered with mats, so I can go wherever I want, whenever I want, as fast as I want." He turned to the hapless medicine man and

ordered: "Have it done by the full moon – or else!" Then he strode back to his teepee and would not be coaxed out.

The medicine man asked the tribeswomen to prepare animal skins at top speed and commanded every last brave to help spread them out over the earth. And the day before the full moon, the medicine man went nervously to the chief's teepee and told him it was done.

"Humph!" grunted the chief and hid a

smile. He stepped out of his teepee and surveyed the skins covering the earth in all directions, as far as he could see. He called for a hunt the very next day, so he could enjoy running as fast and as far as he liked.

Of course, it was impossible for the skins to cover the earth entirely. The swift-footed chief didn't notice where the skins finished, and stepped straight into a patch of thorns. He howled with pain and rage.

Back in the village, the furious chief raged at his unfortunate medicine man: "You have failed me. Tomorrow you will meet your fate."

But by morning, the desperate medicine man had come up with his best idea yet – he had made what looked like two small leather canoes. Trembling, he knelt before the chief and eased them over his feet.

They felt snug. They felt warm. They felt comfortable.

Suddenly, the chief got the idea.

"Humph!" he grunted and hid a smile as he stood up. He took one step. Then another. Then he strode away, beaming.

And from that day onwards, all the Native American people wore moccasins.

How the Camel got his Hump

Adapted from the story by Rudyard Kipling

In the beginning of years, when the world was so new and all, and the Animals were just beginning to work for Man, there was a Camel. He lived in the middle of a Howling Desert and he did not want to work. So he ate sticks and thorns and tamarisks and milkweed and prickles, most 'scruciating idle, and when anybody spoke to him he said "Humph!" Just "Humph!" and no more.

Presently the Horse came to him on Monday morning, with a saddle on his back and a bit in his mouth, and said, "Camel, O Camel, come out and trot like the rest of us."

"Humph!" said the Camel, and the Horse went away and told the Man.

Presently the Dog came to him with a stick in his mouth, and said, "Camel, O Camel, come and fetch and carry like the rest of us."

"Humph!" said the Camel, and the Dog went away and told the Man.

Presently the Ox came to him, with the yoke on his neck and said, "Camel, O Camel, come out and plough like the rest of us."

"Humph!" said the Camel, and the Ox went away and told the Man.

At the end of the day the Man called the Horse and the Dog and the Ox together, and said, "Three, O Three, I'm very sorry for you (with the world so new-and-all), but that Humph-thing in the Desert can't work or he would have been here by now, so I am going to leave him alone, and you must work double-time to make up for it."

That made the Three very angry (with the world so new-and-all), and they held a pow-wow on the edge of the Desert. The Camel came along chewing on milkweed most 'scruciating idle, and laughed at them. Then he said "Humph!" and went away again.

Presently there came along the Djinn in charge of All Deserts, in a rolling cloud of dust (Djinns always travel that way because it is Magic), and he stopped to pow-wow with the Three.

"Djinn of All Deserts," said the Horse, "is it right for anyone to be idle, with the world so new-and-all?"

"Certainly not," said the Djinn.

"Well," said the Horse, "there's a thing in the middle of your Howling Desert with a long neck and long legs, and he hasn't done a stroke of work since Monday morning. He won't trot."

"Whew!" said the Djinn, whistling. "That's my Camel, for all the gold in Arabia! What does he say about it?"

"He says 'Humph!'" said the Dog. "And he won't fetch and carry."

"Does he say anything else?"

"Only 'Humph!' – and he won't plough," said the Ox.

"Very good," said the Djinn. "I'll 'humph' him, if you will kindly wait just a minute."

The Djinn rolled himself up in his dust-cloak and took a bearing across the desert, and found the Camel most 'scruciatingly idle, looking at his own reflection in a pool of water.

"My long and bubbling friend," said the Djinn, "what's this I hear of your doing no work, with the world so new-and-all?"

"Humph!" said the Camel.

The Djinn sat down with his chin in his hand, and began to think a Great Magic, while the Camel looked at his own reflection in the pool of water.

"You've given the Three extra work ever since Monday morning, all on account of your 'scruciating idleness," said the Djinn, and with his chin in his hand he

383

went on thinking Magics.

"Humph!" said the Camel.

"I shouldn't say that again if I were you," said the Djinn. "Bubbles, I want you to work."

The Camel said "Humph!" again. No sooner had he said it than he saw his smooth back, which he was so proud of, puffing up and puffing up into a great big lolloping humph.

"Do you see that?" said the Djinn. "That's your very own humph that you've brought upon your very own self by not working. Today is Thursday, and you've done no work since Monday, when the work began. Now you are going to work."

"How can I," said the Camel, "with this

humph on my back?"

"That has a purpose," said the Djinn, "all because you missed those three days. You will be able to work now for three days without eating, because you can live off your humph – and don't you ever say I never did anything for you. Come out of the Desert and go to the Three, and behave. Humph yourself!"

So, humph and all, the Camel humphed himself away to join the Three. And from that day to this the Camel always wears a humph – although we call it a 'hump' now, so we don't hurt his feelings.

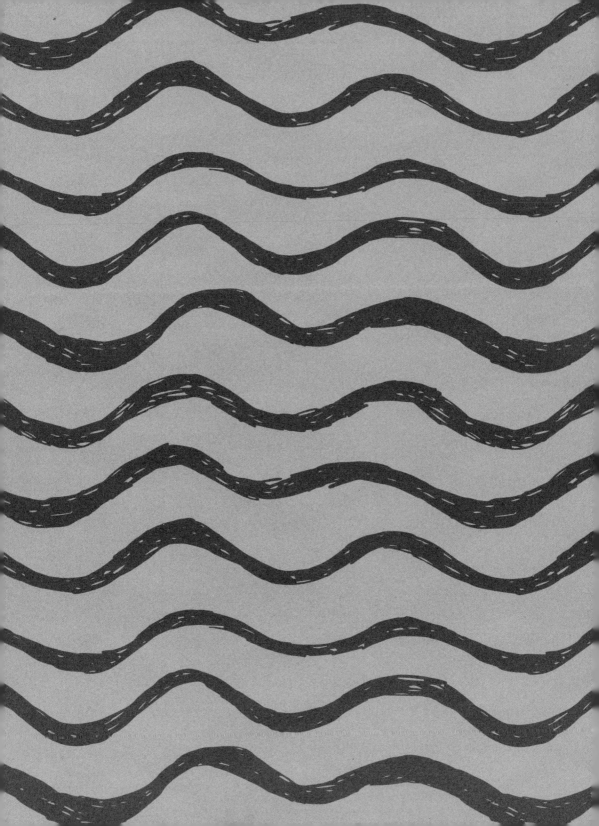